THE TRAIN
TO WARSAW

THE TRAIN
TO WARSAW

A Novel

Gwen Edelman

Grove Press
New York

Printed in the United States of America
Published simultaneously in Canada

ISBN: 978-0-8021-2244-5
eBook ISBN: 978-0-8021-9264-6

Grove Press
an imprint of Grove/Atlantic, Inc.
154 West 14th Street
New York, NY 10011

Distributed by Publishers Group West

www.groveatlantic.com

14 15 16   10 9 8 7 6 5 4 3 2 1

For
Jakov Lind

THE TRAIN
TO WARSAW

The train to Warsaw traveled into the snowy landscape. The sky hung white and motionless above the earth and a pale thin light shone on the snow. Once in a while the bare branches of a tree became visible beneath the snow. And once they saw a bird with black wings as he perched on a snowy limb.

She sat wrapped in a heavy coat, a fur hat pulled over her hair, staring out at the snow covered fields rushing past. Look, she said, pointing a gloved finger, there's a bird who has forgotten to fly south. He sat opposite her in the closed compartment, smoking his black tobacco. He wore a thick scarf wrapped around his neck. His wavy white hair rose up off his forehead like a prophet. Just like the Jews, he remarked. They didn't fly off when they still could. He pulled a flake of tobacco from his tongue. And then it was too late. They should have learned from the birds. Were we any better? she asked. We did what we could, he replied.

He pulled back the stiff pleated curtain that hung from the window and his dark eyes peered out. This frozen landscape makes me melancholy, he said. There is nothing human in it. She stared out, her head tilted as though listening. I did not think, she said, that I would see this landscape again. This endless snow. How beautiful it is. The whole world white and unbroken.

She rubbed with a gloved finger at the condensation. Everything is frozen. I remember that. And that pale light. We wore fur lined boots, and doeskin gloves. And went sledding in the Saxony Gardens. When you still could, he remarked. Please, Jascha, don't ruin it for me. Ruin it for you? he asked. Wasn't it the Others who did that? She stared out the window. In all this whiteness, I can't tell where the sky ends and the earth begins, she said.

He fiddled with the small metal ashtray, attempting to pull it out. Are we a race of birds, he asked, that we are expected to use these tiny ashtrays? He frowned and his lips tightened as he tugged at it. It's going to come out, she warned him. But he continued to pull angrily and suddenly the ashtray tore loose from the wall below the window, scattering tobacco and ashes. She shook her head. You haven't changed. It serves them right if I grind my cigarettes out on the floor, he said, and his face took on a reckless expression. She leaned over to pick up the ashtray and reinsert it. Still as stubborn and impatient, she remarked, as you were Back There.

Now as they sat together in the freezing compartment, he said to her: I'm very angry with you. Did I not tell you I wouldn't go back? But you nagged me and nagged me. He pulled up the collar of his coat. Don't they heat these trains? he asked irritably. Do you by any chance remember the Garden of Eden? How Eve nagged him night and day until at last he ate of the fruit. And we know what happened then. We have long ago left the Garden of Eden, she replied. It's our last chance, she said. If we don't go back now, we never will. Why go back at all? he wanted to know. Didn't we have enough of it Back There?

Out the window the wind shook the pine trees and the snow spun off in powdered waves. Look how slender the birches are, she said to him. They look as though they would crack beneath the weight of the snow, but they don't. God made the birches in Poland to withstand everything, he told her. He knew a birch in Poland would not have it easy. Lilka gazed out the window. There wasn't a bird or a leaf, she said. If there were we would have eaten it. All the trees and all the birds had fled to The Other Side. And inside there was us. Shut up behind high walls. And it seemed as though all of life was on The Other Side. I dreamed of trees and birds, then and later. They appear to me in all shapes and forms, and often they speak to me in a language I seem to understand. But then the leaves drop off one by one and all that is left are bare branches. She shrugged. Polish winter.

They smoked silently. Nearly forty years have passed, she said at last. She removed her fur hat and ran her fingers through her blonde hair. He ground out his cigarette. You still "look good" as we used to say Back There, he remarked. You still look Polish. Where did you get those blue eyes and flaxen hair? Did your grandmother lie down with a Ukrainian peasant in the heat of the day? She sighed. You've asked me that a hundred times. Have I? He laughed. Give me your hand, darling. Let me kiss it.

The seats were of worn maroon plush and the small white antimacassars on the backs were yellowed with age. When they shifted in their seats the springs cried out. The stiff curtain at the window rocked with the movement of the train. Lilka reached into her purse. She pulled out a lipstick and a small mirror and carefully applied red lipstick. After the war, she said, I found a red lipstick someone had left on a train seat. I wiped it off and put on the lipstick. My lips were gleaming red. When I looked at myself I thought how cheerful I looked, how festive. And I thought that if

I wore it all the time, they wouldn't notice how thin my face had become. My bones stuck out then and my cheeks were hollow. Women who were not born then try to look like that. She shook her head. They understand nothing. Well never mind, she said and put away the lipstick.

The faces of the starving became like masks, he said. He ground out his cigarette and lit another. She drew off her gloves and lit a cigarette. Please, Jascha, she said with a frown. Don't frown, darling, he said. It makes you look older.

The compartment grew heavy with smoke. The white light from outside turned the rising whorls bluish and a haze fell over them. When we get to Warsaw, said Lilka, I want to walk in the Saxony Gardens. The swans won't be there in this cold, but even so . . . She grew animated. My parents used to take me to the Saxony Gardens every Sunday. My father would put me on his lap after we had fed bread to the swans and imitate the sounds of animals. A cat, a mouse, a cow, a duck.

There was your father, my mother told me, squeaking and quacking and mooing. I told him he would scare you—you were so small. But it made you laugh. Lilka's cheeks grew shiny. He used to let me watch him shave. I was three or four. And he would dip his finger into his shaving cup and put a little dab on my nose and sing me a little song. Today I bake, tomorrow I brew, and Rumpelstiltskin is my name . . .

I know about Rumpelstiltskin, said Jascha. He didn't want anyone to guess his real name. Just like the Jews. But one day in the forest he pronounced his name out loud and that was the end of everything. He blew smoke rings into the air. Just like the Jews.

In the Saxony Gardens, he said, I used to watch couples coupling in the shadows cast by the bushes. Once when I came too close, drawn by the patch of glistening pink skin where the girl's skirt had ridden up, he shouted at me to get lost. The girl raised her head for a moment and laughed. He's a child, she said. He wants to learn. Let him learn somewhere else, said the man, and he pulled at her skirt. But in a moment he had forgotten me and was pumping away.

Is that how you learned what it was all about? Not at all, he replied. I tore the relevant pages from my parents' medical encyclopedia and took them to school. There I charged money to let the other boys have a look. It was clinical, but informative. My parents never missed them. It seems they did not consult those particular pages. I had them with me until I left home. By then I was tired of them. How often could I study anatomical drawings of the sex organs? Besides, by then I had seen the real thing. He dropped his cigarette on the floor.

No Jew could set foot in the Saxony Gardens, said Jascha, don't you remember? Or in any other gardens. She looked at him. Why do you tell me this now? she asked. Was I not there? Ach, Jascha, you want to ruin it for me. Is that how you see it? he asked. London is not my home, she said.

Even after forty years, London is as alien to me as the other side of the moon. The sky is alien to me. The streets, the houses, the landscape, the food, the voices. And most of all, the faces . . .

Jascha, she pleaded, I want to go home. He shook his head. My poor darling, he said. Do you think that going back will take you home again? He reached forward and took her hand in his. Lilka my angel, he said, let us eat chocolates and forget all this. Give me the one with the cherry liqueur, he said and held out his hand. And what if that is the one I want? she asked coquettishly, shaking out her hair. Light me another cigarette, she said. One of mine. I don't want your dreadful Russian ones. I like them, he said. They remind me of *mahorka,* that foul black tobacco the Russians brought at the end of the war. He took out one of her English cigarettes and lit it for her. Black as night and dense as pitch. But I got used to the taste. And now I can't do without it.

The train flew through the snow, throwing up snowy spray as it went, scattering the wildlife that came near and flew or hopped or ran from the oncoming train. On what day did God create snow? asked Jascha, looking out the window. On the same day He created Poland, replied Lilka. He leaned forward and touched her cheek. What a sweetheart you are, he said.

He drew out a dented and tarnished silver flask from his pocket. Where did that come from? she asked. He smiled. I found it in one of my snow boots, which I haven't used since the last time it snowed in London, a hundred years ago. Let me see, she said, reaching out a hand. First let me drink, darling. He took a long drink and offered it to her. She stared at it. Jascha, this is from Back There.

I found it in an empty apartment, he said. They weren't coming back. Why shouldn't I have it? Instead of the Germans or the Ukrainians. I had it with me all the time. I began to feel it was keeping me alive. What was in it, you mean, she said. No, he replied. The little flask itself. She held it gingerly and gave it back. It's strange to see it after all this time. An artifact from another lifetime. He looked at her. That's what I've been trying to tell you, darling. Another lifetime. You won't find your way back. God knows why we're going, he added. Didn't we have enough?

Jascha stared out the window. When Dante was exiled, he said, what he missed more than anything was the taste of his own bread. Tuscan bread had no salt. For Dante, the bread of exile was unbearably salty. How unhappy he was. Jascha handed her the flask. Have a sip, darling. Have two. Do you think you are the only one who dreams of home?

She took the flask and drank. The waters of forgetting, she said, wiping her mouth with a white lace handkerchief. He smiled. Look at you. Where did you get those manners? Like a Polish countess.

It's freezing in here, she said. Can't they heat these trains? Look, she said and pointed to the steamy breath that rose up before her face. It will be worse when we pass the Polish border, he said. The temperature will drop and there will be icicles in our hair. Let me sit beside you, she said softly.

The light was fading, the slender birches wreathed in shadows. The compartment grew darker. I remember this, he said. The Polish darkness that comes on in winter at three in the afternoon. Our parents called to us from upstairs windows to come in, but we stayed out in the darkness playing as long as we could. There was no curfew then. And no walls. Only our stubborn parents who would not let us play all night. When we grow up, we thought, we'll be free. Ha. What did we know?

You never talk about your parents, she said. No, he said curtly. I can't.

He rolled a cigarette and blew smoke rings into the airless compartment. The smoky wreaths balanced motionless for a moment and then dissolved. It was a gray and overcast day when I came to London, he said.

A choppy crossing. The gulls shrieked above the black water, the passengers were pale with seasickness. A sickly moon hung in the noontime sky as the ship drew near the wooden pier with its rotten timbers. Under my arm I carried my manuscript, written on pages of waxy butcher's paper and tied up with butcher's string. It might have encircled a flank steak, a leg, a neck. Instead I wound it around the packet of words, written in tiny script to save space.

We disembarked. There were men in faded uniforms with creased and tired faces feeding on some kind of soft roll. Everything was colorless. Where have I come to? Is this the end of my wanderings? This dismal and colorless island? I did not want to get off. I had made a mistake. I couldn't live in a place like this. Particularly without you. But you had disappeared.

Now in London the words streamed out of me. I couldn't sleep. I worked day and night. And every day I walked several miles to see whether there was a response to the little card I had put up on the bulletin board at the International Refugee Organization. I couldn't afford a bus, and my shoes were too tight. So I took them off. I tied the laces together and hung them around my neck and walked barefoot through the streets of London. The desert of London. It was almost biblical, my search for you. Was it possible that you were no more? Let's not talk about that now, she said.

We had made a plan, he said. But you didn't come. Stop it, Jascha, she replied. It wasn't like that.

When I came to London at the end of the war, said Lilka, I was exhausted. I could barely move my arms and legs. I found myself among people who were incomprehensible. I spoke good English. And yet I understood nothing. Neither the words, nor the gestures, nor the expressions. Were these pale colorless people happy or sad, angry or ecstatic? Who could tell? I was at sea, lost among these unexpressive people. On that gray island it was all the same.

I wanted to shake them. Yes madam, no madam, they said smilingly, and my heart sank at their sweet, meaningless manners. Where have I come to? I wondered. And at night I dreamed of places where people laughed and cried, shook their fists, threw up their hands, and moaned with pleasure. It was all as bland as the bland white fish they ate in every pub and tavern. I was in exile from all the colors and sounds of life as I knew it. How would I live? Her chest rose and fell. He stared at her out of dark eyes. Are you telling me?

He ground out his cigarette. Once upon a time, I too thought I would go back. But I soon understood how absurd my longing was. Do you not know, he said, that the sages counsel us not to look back over an abyss we have crossed. Do you remember Lot's wife who looked back? The poor woman was turned to salt. Fit only for deer to lick.

Lilka went into her purse and took out a handful of individually wrapped chocolates. She held them out to him. Have a sweet, she said. He leaned forward to take one and she ruffled his hair. You know I don't like to be stroked, he said sharply. I'm not a dog.

There was a knock at the door to the compartment and they stiffened. A small hunched man in a loose-fitting porter's uniform slid open the door. His face was crumpled, pale strands of hair crossed his scalp. *Meine Damen und Herren,* he said. He pointed at his small cart with pastries resting on white paper doilies. The pastries looked hard and inedible. Lilka leaned forward. That one, she said in German. The chocolate one. She smiled happily. And hot chocolate. He laid the pastry on a plate and set a fork alongside. The chocolate icing on the éclair looked dusty.

I call this train the Siberia Express, the man said, rearranging the pastries. They barely heat it. And then they expect me to wear this flimsy uniform. No coat, no scarf. He shook his head. When I get home I'm frozen like an ice cube. He poured out the hot chocolate. This used to be my favorite, he remarked. Now it's brandy. And you, sir? I want a coffee and an almond pastry, said Jascha in English. Where are you from, sir? asked the man. Jascha reached in his pocket and brought out his wallet. How much? he asked curtly. The man gave him the figure in English. Now he seemed in a hurry to leave, and thanking them, he rapidly shut the door.

What was the point of that? she asked him. He was a harmless creature. Why do you behave like that? I cannot stand, he said, to hear that Berlin accent. And I'm tired of people asking me where I'm from. But they always do, she said. Wherever we go. She sipped at the hot chocolate. It's lukewarm. She took a bite of the pastry. And this is hard as rock. What did you expect? he asked.

The snowy fields lay in shadow, a pale sliver of moon rose over the snow. I'm starving, he said. She brushed her hair. I'm going to order venison. And wash it down with Polish vodka. My sweetheart, this is not the Hotel Bristol, he informed her. But I will buy you a venison dinner in Warsaw. Now that I can, he added.

Do you suppose the dining car is open? she asked. She
pulled another chocolate from her purse. I'm ravenous,
she whispered. What shall we eat? What shall we eat?
he replied. We'll have cabbage and pierogi, latkes and
goose liver, roasted potatoes and duck dripping with fat
and drowning in sour cherry sauce. We'll mop it all up
with black bread and finish off with Black Forest cake.
What won't we have? She smiled. How delicious. Jascha, she said happily, we'll have a banquet. A banquet
in the ruins, he replied. Jascha! No darling, he said,
just a banquet.

They put on their fur hats and re-buttoned their coats.
He put his hand beneath her arm. Come my sweetheart, let me escort you. Now even Jews can dine in
first class dining cars.

———

It happened that when the leaves on the trees turned
red and gold, Jascha received a letter from Poland. It
lay on the hall table in their house in London, a cream
colored envelope with a Polish stamp. Jascha looked

at it. What is this? he asked. News from Poland after forty years? The news can only be bad. And he left it lying there. Open it, Lilka had said. No, darling, he replied, better not. She reached for the envelope. He put a warning hand on her wrist. Let me, she said softly. What's the harm?

She pulled out a cream colored card. It's an invitation, she informed him.

An invitation? he asked. Do they miss their Jews? Are they inviting us back after all these years? Come back, dear Jews? And in writing! She read from the stiff card written in a Polish hand.

To Mr. Jascha Kroll: We invite you, our esteemed Polish writer, to honor us with a reading of your work at Writers' House in Warsaw on December 9th. We shall be happy to welcome you back and look forward to the honor of having you with us at Writers' House. With cocktails and a light buffet to follow.

Jascha went to the freezer and took out a bottle of vodka. Ha, he said, slamming the door. First they want me dead. Now I'm a native son, an "esteemed Polish writer." Who will come to this reading, I wonder? He poured out the vodka into two shot glasses. Three spinster schoolteachers, a couple of birds, six dead Jews? What chutzpah. They haven't changed.

They sat together at the round wooden table covered in a dark red cloth. Why shouldn't we go? asked Lilka. Her thin silver bangles clinked as she raised her glass. I want them to know what a great writer they lost. Who writes in Polish. Who speaks to them of all they would like to forget. And do you think, he asked, that they will want to be reminded? When you read from your books, they'll be reminded. Reminded? he asked. They'll run off into the snowy night. They won't sleep for a week. We didn't sleep for four years, she remarked, and lifting her throat she drank back the vodka.

I'm not going back to that hellhole, he told her. Not for anything. Not if you paid me. Not if Churchill took me by the hand. Write and tell them that. December? he asked in disbelief. When all of Poland lies frozen beneath the snow? When the wind sings in the chimneys and the water freezes in the pipes? Well the answer is no. You can tell them that. But Jascha, it's our last chance. Soon it will be too late. Why? he asked. Are we leaving for the next world? She shrugged. We're no longer young. Speak for yourself, he said. We'll go for three days, she said. What can happen? Many things, he replied. The war is over, she told him. It's not the same Warsaw. Is it not the same Poles? he asked.

You'll read to them from your brilliant books, said Lilka. What's the harm? He studied her as she drank. It's you who wants to go back, you sly witch. Why don't you say so? She took up the small wooden bird that sat on the table. Maybe I do, she said at last.

The room was in near darkness. What are we getting to eat? he asked. I'm starving. She got up and turned on the lamp. I couldn't face cooking, she replied, so everything is cold. He lit a cigarette. Cold leftovers, he said mournfully. Once upon a time you cooked for me every night. This is what happens. Women lose interest. There was a time when your dearest desire was to spend hours cooking me my favorite things. I could say the same, she replied. You used to bring me stockings with a black seam up the back. You brought me chocolates. And pink soaps tied up in little packages. And now? Do you still want all that? he asked. She shrugged. Yes. No.

She set the table and brought plates of smoked salmon and dark bread, potato salad, beet salad, sour cream, lemons, a pot of butter, and the frosted bottle of vodka. He poured out two more shots of vodka. And spooned out a large serving of beet salad for her. Your beloved beets, he said. That's the peasant in you. And you, she said, bending forward to light the candles, with your coarse black bread and your herring.

Jascha raised his glass. Let us drink to two refugees from the former city of Warsaw, he said. Sometimes late at night they remember the trees, the bread, the birds of their native land, and the soft sounds of their own language.

She pressed back her blonde hair and raised her glass. Let us drink to our return, she proposed. We'll go back. No darling, he replied. We won't. Outside a dog barked. Look at you, he said, your mouth is red with beet stain. Just like children in Poland before the war. When they harvested the beets the children's faces were red with the juice of beets. Wipe your mouth my sweetheart, I don't want to think about it.

He smoked and ate at the same time. She helped herself to another forkful of beets. I'm the only woman who would put up with the smell of that tobacco, she said. Quite a few others did, he said. I doubt it, she said, chewing slowly, you're too difficult. He smiled. But that's what women love, my sweetheart. She cut into the dark bread and placed a slice of smoked salmon on top. Don't speak to me, she said. He laughed. What a crazy woman, he said, his mouth full.

I dream of Warsaw all the time, she told him. Some-times it is closer to me than anything. She pried open the jar. Just once more, she said, lifting a herring out delicately from the brine, I would like to see the street where I lived when I was a girl. She placed the herring on a piece of rye bread, added a thin slice of onion and handed it to him. Is that so terrible?

Lilka placed another herring on a piece of bread and pressed it into her mouth. If my mother could see me eating like this, she said with a laugh. Who did she think she was? asked Jascha. The Countess Razumovsky?

In Warsaw I want to walk down Marszałkowska, she said. Where we used to stroll before the war. And stop to look in the shop windows. My father wore his coat with the fur collar. My mother wore a small black velvet hat with a veil. I remember, she said, when the wind shifted and the scent of pines blew in from the Praga forests. And all of Warsaw smelled like a pine forest. His mouth tightened. When the wind shifted the smell of burning gagged us, he said, the place was rubble, the sky was black with ash, the facades had crumbled and the streets were full of corpses. That's your precious Warsaw. She turned her face away. Why do you ruin it for me?

Your beloved Warsaw is ashes and rubble, he said. There's nothing left. Not a building, not a house, not a street that remains from before. Everything you knew is gone. Burned. Finished. Kaput. Forget your idea of going back. Have they changed the sky? she asked, her cheeks flushed. The air? Has the Vistula changed course? He sighed. My darling, you sound like a schoolgirl. Ach, Lilka. Poland is a morgue.

Her thin bangle bracelets clinked against each other. Then I'll go alone. Ha, he replied. Let you return to Poland on your own? Let you wander in the kingdom of the dead on your own? How could I? I would have to come and rescue you. Oh Jascha, don't be so silly. It is no longer allowed to pull the earlocks of Jews in the third class carriages, he said. Nevertheless even now, forty years later, it is hardly a child's garden of verses in our beloved homeland.

The radiator clanked and the heat began to rise with a hiss. Lilka brought out a small chocolate cake. Is it the one I like? he asked. She nodded. With marzipan? His eyes grew shiny. Oh darling, he said. Come and sit on my lap. Let me hug you and kiss you. I'll take you to Paris. We'll go to Fouquet's. I'll buy you stockings with a black seam up the back. Like before the war. I don't want to go to Paris, she said. Take me to Warsaw.

She cut the cake into paper thin slices. He watched her. Do you think you are still Back There? Are you saving a sliver for tomorrow and another for the day after? She put one of the slices in her mouth and then another. Will you hide one under your scarf? he asked. Another in your underwear? Leave me alone, she said.

I'm going to call Warsaw tomorrow, she said. Call the ghetto telephone, he said. I still remember the number.

I'm not staying in the ghetto. I'm going to stay at the Hotel Bristol, she said, chewing her cake. What? he cried. The most expensive hotel in Warsaw? And who may I ask will pay for that? I will, she said, licking her fork. You're crazy, he said. Where will you get that kind of money? I will get it, she said. He watched her. What a sweet girl, one might think. But behind that blonde hair, those big blue eyes, and goyish face lies Judah Maccabee. And who did I learn it from? she wanted to know. From you, my angel. She served them both another slice of cake. Eat, she said. Now that we can.

Many nights they dreamed of food. They saw loaves of dark rye bread flying through the air, pails of cherries spilling out on the ground, piles of shiny apples, tables of endless cakes, buckets of chocolates. In waking life the refrigerator had always to be full of food, the shelves stuffed with all manner of canned goods. God forbid, he said, that we should run out of food. They kept chocolate bars in the drawers of their night tables. And often during the night they got up and came into the kitchen in their nightclothes and sat down for an entire meal as the stars shone down on them from the black night sky.

I dreamed that I was hungry, he would tell her as he ate eagerly. I dreamed that I was dying of thirst, she would say. Who else could we live with if not each other? he would ask. Who else could understand?

After dinner they would go out for a walk or to the casino. He was too restless to work at night. It was in the afternoon that he struggled with his stories in the room at the end of the hall. Once upon a time the words had poured out of him and he had become famous. Now, he told her, I cannot find my way. So many stories. But I seem to have lost access to all that. As though it were all buried deep within the earth and I cannot dig it out . . .

Many years ago, Lilka told him, Hagar was wandering in the desert with her small son Ishmael. There was no water. They walked and walked. Soon they would die of thirst. Hagar prayed to God for help. And He answered her. Hagar, look, He said. The well is in front of your eyes. And she saw that it was. Jascha turned to her in surprise. Where did you learn that? From you, she replied.

Near midnight when the moon rocked in the night sky, he said to her: brush your feathers, darling, *schnell schnell*. We're going to try our luck at the tables. Several times a week they went out to the casino. Often they stayed until three or four in the morning. Sometimes as they walked home, the sky had already begun to lighten in the east. Now they walked through the darkened London streets, still slick with rain. It will soon be winter, she said, pulling her coat tightly around her. Why won't you wear a coat, you stubborn man?

They came to a black door and rang the bell. Inside they showed their passports to a broad shouldered man and were buzzed through to the gaming room. Let me see, she said and reached for his passport. Inside the Polish passport with the golden eagle was the photo of a much younger man. I forgot how handsome you were, she said. I still am, he replied. Why do you keep this? she asked. You always say that the name and memory of Warsaw should be blotted out. He took back the passport roughly. That's not the whole truth. Now let's go and play.

They sat together at the table covered in green felt with squares of red and black. Shaded lamps illuminated the numbers. Beyond the tables the room lay in darkness. Tonight I'm feeling reckless, Lilka said, and she placed a stack of chips on the 28. You're getting a bit too reckless, he remarked, eyeing the stack. Never mind, she said gaily, I'm going to win tonight. And if I win on the 28, you'll come to Poland. Who says so? he asked. *Faites vos jeux,* called out the croupier. *Rien ne va plus.*

This is where I feel at home, he would tell her. Here there is no time or space, no day or night. All your problems disappear and only the numbers exist. Unlike her, he took risks. He would place a large pile of chips on one number and then put them on the same number again. And again. Numbers are mystical, he told her. Each has a meaning. When I look at the numbers on the felt, I remember my ancestors who understood the universe that separated the 3 from the 4. He sat at the table, smoking continuously, intent on the silver wheel as it spun round and round. At those moments she couldn't talk to him.

When he won, he was happy and all of life seemed good. When he lost, shadows appeared beneath his eyes and the end of the world seemed imminent. Why do you get so worked up each time the ball drops into the slot? As though your life depended on it? she asked him. It does, you silly girl, he replied and blew out a cloud of that foul black tobacco. From one second to the next, your fortunes change—just like during the war.

He inhaled deeply and blew out small smoke rings. Winston Churchill said: play for more than you can afford to lose and you will learn the game. That's me. He let slide a stack of blue chips onto the 7. During the war you could disappear from one moment to the next.

A turn of the wheel and it was all over. Lovemaking was never as good as when you might die in the next moment. A girl's soft thighs were never as enticing as when they might disappear from one moment to the next. Only the casino where you can lose everything from one moment to the next reminds me of that other life. A girl's? she said. What girl?

At the end of a losing streak she would plead with him not to put any more money down. I'll get it back, he would say. At the last moment, when all seems lost, the earth spins on its axis, your luck changes, and you win it back. And sometimes he did. When he won big, they would go to the bar and order champagne. And he would slide his hand up her leg and ask if they should do it right there. On top of the bar. Let them see, he crowed. What do we care? We've won!

Again and again the long thin wrist of the croupier shot out from the white cuff and spun the wheel. Lilka placed another stack of chips on the 28. Sorry, darling, he said as her stack was raked off the table. Lilka carefully counted out thirty chips and placed them once again on the 28. Third time lucky, she said. Light me a cigarette. Stop, Lilka, what's gotten into you? You're playing like me. And he reached out to take back her chips. Leave them there, she warned. The wheel began to spin and she leaned forward to watch. As the wheel spun, the light glinted off the silver grooves, the black and red numbers blurred. Lilka watched, motionless. Now the wheel slowed at last. The silver ball rocked and nearly fell into the 29. *Proszę proszę,* she murmured. Please please. The ball hesitated for a split second and then dropped with a click into the 28. She turned to him triumphantly. Jascha, I've won! Straight up. On a number. Thirty-five to one—750 pounds! She laughed happily as the croupier's rake pushed toward her the high stacks of chips. Did I not tell you? I invite you, she said, to three nights at the Hotel Bristol. In the former city of Warsaw.

They walked home through the dark rain slick streets. It was meant to be, she informed him. Ach Lilka. So superstitious. Like everyone Back There. One woman saw the word Gęsia Street written on a sheet of newsprint and was convinced that the next roundup would be on Gęsia Street. Nearly everyone saw a significance in numbers. If they suddenly saw the number seven written somewhere it meant trouble in seven days. Or there would be a raid at #7 on some street or another. And so on. If there is a crazier way to predict the future, I would like to know it. Don't be so harsh, she said. When you are that helpless, why not tether yourself to a number? What else is there to cling to? Are you now a philosopher? he asked.

She took his arm. Come back to Warsaw with me, my Jascha. When have I ever asked you for anything? She stared at him. Well, once. And I gave her up, didn't I? he replied.

Two days later she went to get the tickets. How many did you get? he asked her.

That night, as the dog across the garden howled at the moon, she began to pull her clothes off the hangers and fold them into a suitcase. I'm coming, he said. And he threw two sweaters into the suitcase. Why do you do this to me? I want to return to Warsaw like I want the cholera, he informed her, and threw in a pair of socks. In the morning they went to the station.

———

In the dining car the tables were spread with dingy white cloths, there were white plates with faded silver rims and dull metal cutlery. Only a third of the tables were occupied. Who goes to Warsaw in winter? said Jascha. Only a madman. A tall bony maitre d' with a long melancholy nose came up to them and indicated a table for two by the window. At a nearby table sat a good-looking man in a double-breasted suit with his dark hair slicked back in the old manner. He examined Lilka as she passed. Unconsciously she lifted a shoulder gracefully. Why do you do that? he asked. Do what? That coquettish gesture of yours when you lift your shoulder. I don't lift my shoulder at all, she said irritably. The maitre d' pulled back her chair and she sat down. He handed them menus. I'm ravenous, she whispered.

Why are you looking at him? he asked. I'm looking at everybody, she replied. I want to see who our fellow passengers are. I'll tell you who they are, he said, they're traveling salesmen. All of them? Most likely. They spend their lives on trains, carrying their heavy sample bags, doing a bit of currency speculation on the side, and bringing a little thrill to lonely housewives all over Eastern Europe.

That man for example, he said, pointing to the one who had watched her. He has three different housewives along the line. In Berlin, on the border in Rzepin, and across the Polish border in Kalisz. But they must buy first before any fun. Those are the rules. They sit together on her couch and examine the merchandise together as he runs a hand smoothly up her leg and she squeals. She shook her head. With you, everything is a story. And why not? he wanted to know. How else will we entertain ourselves on endless train rides?

The waiter appeared, a ruddy-faced man whose uniform was too big, carrying oversize menus. *Polski?* he asked. English, said Jascha. The man looked at him in surprise. Very well, sir. What is it you are wanting?

There was no venison, only some whitish pork chops served with a tasteless gravy. She put down her fork. I'm ready for dessert.

He poured out more shots from the bottle of Polish vodka that stood on the table. At least that hasn't changed, she remarked. The dining car swayed and they heard the shrieking of the wind outside. Jascha looked at his watch. We will be at the border in half an hour, he told her. Let's order some chocolate cake, she suggested, to cheer us up. He refilled their glasses. She laughed. Jascha, she said loudly, soon I won't be able to stand up.

They made their way back to their compartment, weaving as they walked. The train was half empty. They passed a Polish family who sat squeezed together. The mother had laid newspaper over her lap and was carving slices of dark sausage onto chunks of bread. Her husband and children waited impatiently, reaching out stubby fingers, talking all at the same time.

Farther on, an old man lay with his head back against the seat, his mouth open, the skin stretched over the bones of his face. Lilka shuddered. A group of sturdy businessmen in suits that strained at the seams sat together smoking, drawing diagrams on sheets of paper.

Just before they reached their compartment, they passed through the platform between the cars. As soon as Jascha opened the door, they felt the sudden icy blast of the air and the shriek of the train as it sped through the landscape. In that small space sat an old peasant woman on an upturned bucket. She wore a voluminous wool skirt, her flowered headscarf nearly covered her forehead. The train rattled, her bent figure vibrated, and she muttered to herself in an incomprehensible Polish dialect. We're getting near the border, said Jascha. It's just the Poles now. He turned to her with an ironic smile. We're almost home darling. Jascha, she said warningly.

They came into their compartment and collapsed side by side onto the maroon plush. God, I've had a lot to drink, she said and laid her head against his shoulder. That Polish vodka is no joke. He put his arm around her. Go to sleep, my sweetheart, he said. When you wake up we'll be in Poland. He leaned his head back against the seat and closed his eyes. Her head dropped onto his shoulder. And there, not far from the Polish border, they fell asleep.

They were awakened as the train ground to a sudden halt. Jascha sat up and looked out in alarm. He gripped her arm. We're here. Lilka awoke with a cry. I can't get out, she cried. It's like a coffin in here. Open the gate, open the gate, the wagon is coming. He shook her. That's enough. Wake up. It's only a dream. The gate, she called out. They've closed the gate. She opened her eyes and stared at him unseeing. I was standing in line. And then I saw that they were closing the gates. We pressed toward the gate but there was no way through. And then the snow began to fall. Stop it Lilka, he said. We're at the border.

She sat up straight and pushed back her hair. She peered out the window. A white sign dusted with snow proclaimed in Russian and Polish and German: You Are Entering Poland. They still have the same huts, she said. Forty years later. They heard the barking of dogs and shouting. She clutched his arm. He sat rigid, looking out the window. What is it? she cried. What's happening?

They stared out the window. In the darkness stood a station attendant in a maroon uniform trimmed in faded gold braid, swinging a lantern that threw faint gleams of yellow light onto the platform. The German shepherds were howling, straining at the leashes held by the men in uniforms. Jascha, she cried, it's not us, is it? He squeezed her arm tightly. No, he hissed. Of course not.

What is happening? she asked. Can you see? Wait, he said. They're taking someone off. A Jew? she whispered. He gripped her arm, his dark eyes cold. Stop this, Lilka, he said. As they watched in the feebly lit darkness, they saw that the police were dragging someone down the steps of the train. She was kicking out her feet in felt boots, her wide skirt ballooned out as they pulled her off. Look at that, said Lilka in surprise. It's the old peasant woman in the headscarf. The woman was screeching at them in high-pitched tones like the squawking of poultry, her kerchief sliding off her skull. The snow fell on her, on the uniforms of the policemen, on the yellowish coats of the dogs. What has she done? cried Lilka. Is she a Jew? The police and the woman disappeared into one of the huts. My God, Jascha, she said wildly, clutching at him. He looked out at her from dark eyes. *Witamy w Polsce,* he said. Welcome to Poland.

It was night when they arrived in Warsaw. They made their way along the icy platform into the terminal. People loaded down with suitcases and parcels rushed past them, bundled up in dark clothes, their pale faces made small by fur hats. Like refugees, remarked Jascha. Lilka stopped. It's not the same station. No, darling, it's not, he agreed. That station was bombed forty years ago. Have you forgotten? The smell of damp woolens and stale cigarette smoke rose in the air. In the fluorescent light young soldiers stood smoking, their faces pale and spotty, their old-fashioned guns hanging off their arms. At least they're not the same uniforms, remarked Jascha. Aren't we lucky?

How drab everyone looks, she said. How dull, how colorless. Can this be Warsaw? Everything was different before the war. And this glaring light, so relentless. That's Communist light, he replied. Where nothing must be hidden. She stood motionless. Jascha, she said, I've gone deaf. I can't hear anything. Everything has gone silent. Come with me, he said. Take my hand. Let us step out into the city that is no more.

In the darkness they stood in line for a taxi. Across the road a streetlamp burned dimly, its light nearly extinguished by the snow. Those in line huddled close together in their padded dark coats and dark fur hats, their heads bent. No one spoke. They can stand in line for hours, for days, murmured Jascha. They've learned to. A sudden bitter icy wind blew through their clothing and froze the skin on their faces. Dear God, said Lilka, hunching her shoulders, her breath emerging in a cloud, I had forgotten how cold it is here. Is this Warsaw? she asked, staring at the square modern buildings. Where has it all gone? Nothing is familiar. Don't worry darling, he said, we'll find something. She looked around. Atop the buildings old-fashioned signs shone dully in the snowy evening. She shivered. Can this be Warsaw? So ugly? So soulless? Jascha, it's another place entirely.

When they were nearly frozen, their turn came. The driver threw their suitcase in the trunk and slammed it shut. They stepped into the old car. The springs groaned as they sat. How much to the Hotel Bristol? asked Jascha. 40 *zlotys,* said the man, his face dark with stubble. That's highway robbery. Jascha, whispered Lilka. We're getting out. Go ahead, replied the driver. Jascha opened the door and a blast of icy air struck them. I can do it for 30, said the man. 15, said Jascha. What is this, a cattle auction? asked the driver. Who would the cattle be? asked Jascha coldly. 17, said Jascha. 20, said the man. Jascha shut the door. All right you thief. I only agree because of my wife, who is tired. Otherwise I wouldn't be so reasonable. The driver turned around to look at Jascha. Jascha stared at him out of dark eyes. What do you do? the driver asked him. What could such a man do for a profession? Jascha smiled coldly. Smuggler, he replied. Jascha, said Lilka, what has come over you? Jascha thrust forward his jaw and smiled. Let them all go to hell, he said softly.

They pulled up at the Bristol. A man in red livery trimmed in gold braid opened the car door. Welcome, he said, and leaned down to extend his hand to Lilka. May I help you, Madame? he asked in Polish. Very kind, replied Lilka. Ah, Madame speaks Polish. Madame is Polish, replied Lilka.

Welcome home, said the doorman with a half bow. His livery was faded, a button was missing, one epaulet had nearly torn free. Jascha emerged from the taxi, his dark eyes glowering beneath his fur *chapka*. The hotel employee stared at him. The gentleman is certainly Polish, he said. He was once, said Jascha. There's a suitcase in the back, he said curtly. He took Lilka by the arm and pulled her into the hotel. And don't steal it, he muttered. They stole everything, said Jascha. Like vultures stripping a carcass. Lilka turned to him. Jascha, she said, stop it. We've only just arrived.

In the once elegant lobby, lit with the white light of fluorescent bulbs, the painted marble of the columns was chipped, the long drapes sagged, the Aubusson carpet was dark with age. Lilka turned to him in dismay. Jascha, she said, what was I thinking? Never mind, he said. It's done now. Go and sit down while I check in.

As she sat with her legs crossed, her blonde hair pulled back tightly, her fur hat in her hand, a man came over to her. He wore a pin-striped suit and his hair was slicked back. He bowed slightly. Does Madame speak Polish? he asked. She looked at him in confusion. What did he want? Identification? Yes, she replied at last. I do. Ah, Madame is Polish, he said. Such a beautiful woman. Might I invite you for a drink in the bar? She shook her head. I'm with my husband. She gestured toward the reception. What a terrible pity, he said. Are you visiting?

Jascha was coming toward them. The man bowed. I wish you a pleasant stay. Who was that oily character? asked Jascha. He wanted to invite me for a drink. What chutzpah, he said. Lilka smiled. What a madman.

A young bellboy took them up in the elevator. His hair was close cropped beneath his small hat and his skin deathly white. He walked quickly down the hall, their old leather suitcase knocking against his thin uniformed leg.

He opened the door. Jascha and Lilka stood at the threshold. *Proszę,* said the boy. Please. And he indicated that they should enter. The bellboy put down their suitcase on the folding luggage rack at the end of the bed. They had not moved. Please, he said again, come in.

———

Who had seen a more beautiful September than the one that struck Warsaw in 1939? The sun rose clear and golden over the city and already early in the morning the warmth lay on your skin. The trees were heavy with leaves, flowers blossomed from pots and trellises on the balconies of apartment buildings. Sunlight streaked the pavements and lay brightly on the stones of the old buildings. Young girls ate grapes greedily from their warm hands, the Azerbaijani vendors were selling lemonade, and sunlight glinted off the choppy surface of the Vistula. For a moment it was good to be alive.

But on September 6th we heard that German panzers were on their way to Warsaw. We prayed that the sunshine would be blotted out. That torrential rainstorms would come and the roads become a sea of impassable mud. And mire all the German tanks and trucks. But the weather remained glorious. Thousands jammed the roads in an exodus from the city. On Monday September 25th at six in the morning the bombardment of Warsaw began. Two days later it was over. Poland had surrendered. Soon it was open season on the Jews.

———

The walls of their room were covered in pale yellow and white stripes. A long white French desk with curved legs edged in gilt stood before one of the windows. A stiff leather folder with hotel stationery lay on top. The large armchair was covered in pale yellow silk and on the walls hung sepia prints of long ago Polish kings with white curls. Elaborate yellow silk curtains, now discolored with age, hung from the long windows. Well well, said Jascha, looking around. He sat down in the armchair in his hat and coat. Lilka sat on the bed. They looked at each other. What shall we do now? she asked. He shrugged. Drink, he replied. What else can we do?

Order a bottle of vodka, she said. And speak Polish for God's sake. She pulled open the drawer in the bedside table and peered in. Here's the New Testament in Polish. In case we need it. You learned the Catholic prayers, didn't you? he remarked. For those unexpected quizzes in the street. Holy Mary, Mother of God, pray for us sinners, now and at the hour of our death, recited Lilka. Marysia taught me when I was a child. She didn't want me to go to hell when I left this world. How about before you left this world? asked Jascha.

He touched the worn silk of the chair. Never in my life did I spend a night in a hotel in Warsaw. My parents would not have understood. Go to a hotel? Like a foreign countess? Like a traveling salesman? Like a whore? Who goes to hotels? What need had we to go to a hotel? asked Lilka. Didn't we have homes of our own? She sat on the bed's high eiderdown and took up a corner of it between her fingers. Real feathers, she said. Like we had before the war.

Jascha lifted the phone and spoke in English. Ach, what a stubborn man. That's what you need, he said. Not some shrinking violet. She shrugged off her coat and leaned down to undo her boots. Well whether I do or not, take off your coat and hat. We're here now.

She got up and went to the window. She peered out into the falling snow lit here and there by muffled lights. I can't see anything, she told him, except the falling snow. Warsaw has disappeared. He went over to the radiator and put his hand on it. There isn't much heat, he remarked. No, she replied. That seems to be a problem everywhere here.

There was a knock at the door and they jumped. Jascha undid the locks. I'll take that, he said, barring the way into the room. He took the tray from the waiter and set it down. There was a bottle of cold vodka, two glasses, a basket of sliced black bread, a pot of butter, and a plate of dill cucumbers. Jascha smiled happily. Look how delicious. He poured out the vodka into small glasses and offered her a slice of buttered bread. She drank. It tastes the same, just as good, she said. You silly girl, he said. Polish vodka will always taste the same. He drank it back and rested his head on the back of the armchair. Why do I feel so sleepy? he asked. As though I could sleep for a hundred years. Suddenly the radiator gave out a clanking sound and a long hiss. The Polish radiator, he said. A work of art in its own right. He took up the bottle and drank. Jascha, why not a glass? Well well, he said. Here we are. Out of the ghetto now. And on The Other Side.

That night as the snow fell on Warsaw, they lay huddled together beneath the high white eiderdown. Far off they heard a church bell ringing out. She pressed her head into his chest and gripped his hand tightly in hers. At last they fell into a restless sleep. In the morning their eyes were dull and reddened. Lilka smoothed her hair back from her damp forehead. Lying in bed, she looked out bleary eyed at the snow falling from a leaden sky. Where have we come to? she asked him.

I dreamed I was Back There, she told him. The snow was falling, just like now. The crowds surged through the narrow streets, the din was deafening. Beggars rode on a wagon piled high with rags, their faces blue with cold, their eyes feverish. In the midst of all that, suddenly I saw my father standing in front of the Wall. He wore his coat with the fur collar. He was hatless. How elegant he looked, his cheeks smooth, his eyes shiny. Papa, I cried, and went toward him. As I came closer, he held out a hand to me. Come with us, he whispered. We are already dead.

Jascha lay on his back smoking. What is that? he asked, pointing up at the shadows on the ceiling. A sparrow? A nightingale? I like birds, he said. When they don't fly, they hop, pressing out their chests like proper Polish officers. She tugged at the soft eiderdown. Why have we come back? Whose idea was it? he asked her.

When I dream of the ghetto in London, she said, at least I am far away. Here I am close enough to touch it. I could walk there in ten minutes. To the ghetto? asked Jascha. It's gone. Have you forgotten? She put a hand to her disheveled hair. But I've ordered a car to take us there this morning. Are you crazy? he asked.

But Jascha, she pleaded, I want to see it one more time. The apartment where I lived when I was a girl. The Jewish Hospital on Stawki Street where I was a nurse-in-training . . . He shifted heavily in the sodden sheets. Lilka, what's the matter with you? he asked. You know as well as I do that those streets have not existed for more than forty years. Cancel the car, he said sharply. We're not going back to that place. How many times do I have to tell you? Every street, every house, every brick, every doorway. It's ashes and rubble.

The radiator clanked with a metallic sound. She lay quietly, her face turned away. Then there's nothing. No, he agreed, there's nothing. He blew his nose into a large white linen handkerchief. Now order some breakfast, he said, I'm starving. I wanted . . . I hoped . . . she began. Yes, darling, he said. Like all of us.

They lay half-asleep, their legs entwined, her head against his chest. There was a knock at the door. Both grew motionless. It's only room service, said Lilka after a moment. She threw on a robe and stood up. A short sturdy man with high cheekbones, straw-colored hair, and unblinking blue eyes pushed a table on wheels into the room. He kicked at a small brake and pulled up two chairs. *Proszę,* he said. Frowning, Jascha pulled on a bathrobe.

They sat opposite each other at the linen covered table. The waiter poured out coffee into china cups whose flowery design had faded with use. Milk and sugar? he asked. He had a square jaw which he pressed out into the middle of the room. We like it black, replied Jascha curtly. It's snowing again, the waiter observed. You can barely see two inches in front of your face. As for the freezing wind, he muttered, the Russkies send it down from the Urals—a special present for the Poles.

The waiter stopped pouring and looked at them with curiosity. We don't get many visitors this time of year. Where are you from? he wanted to know. From London, replied Jascha. He took up the Polish newspaper that lay beside the plate. Where did you learn your Polish? asked the waiter. Jascha studied the headlines. The

waiter stood motionless, staring at Jascha out of his
fixed blue eyes. It's not the same Warsaw, said the man
at last. Jascha pulled out a few coins and handed them
over. Slowly the man looked down into his palm. He
lifted his eyes to Jascha. Have you come back?

What chutzpah, said Jascha. To question us like that.
He snapped the page of the newspaper angrily. They
haven't changed. Still sly and insolent.

Never mind, said Lilka and drew the bread basket
toward her. Do you remember, he asked, when suddenly the waiters and the street sweepers, the brick-
layers and the scum rose up until the lowliest drudge
was higher than all the Jews? That's what my mother
couldn't bear, said Lilka. She wasn't the only one,
replied Jascha.

Lilka, her face creased with sleep, studied the basket
of rolls and selected a poppy-seed roll. It's not even
warm, she said. She broke it open and held it up to

her nose. Jascha, it smells of nothing. Do you remember the freshly baked poppy-seed rolls before the war? Warm and fragrant. Like paradise. Mechanically she buttered the bread and took a bite. No taste. For years I dreamed of biting into a real Warsaw poppy-seed roll. Like they used to bake at Rosenstajn's. Jascha peered into the basket. Well well, he said. Now that the Jews are gone they're baking Jewish pastries. Look at that. Rugelach with raisins. Like my mother used to make. She looked up in surprise. You never talk about your mother. No, he replied.

At Rosenstajn's, said Lilka, the poppy-seed rolls came straight from the oven. You could lie down in that warm fragrant scent. She chewed slowly. The Rosenstajns were husband and wife. She was small and round and had skin as white as flour. My father used to say that was why he chose her. She could have been dark as rye, he remarked. Is that your sense of humor? she asked. No darling, he replied. He turned the pages of the Polish newspaper. I don't have one. Rosenstajn looked something like Houdini, she said. Dark curls, short, and solidly built. But he had delicate fingers.

Sometimes he gave me a little cookie in the shape of
a star. Not that kind of star, she added. His wife used
to bend down and pinch my cheek. Look at that flaxen
hair, she would say. Just like a Polish princess.

He turned a page of the Warsaw paper. Well well, he
remarked. An old woman has been robbed and mur-
dered. Only one? That wasn't news in our day. Where
did it happen? she wanted to know. On Nowolipki
Street, he said. Around midnight. Our Side, said Lilka.
What was she doing out so late? After curfew? He
frowned. What are you talking about?

When the Germans arrived, said Lilka, they soon dis-
covered that it was the best bakery in Warsaw. Later
when the Rosenstajns went to the ghetto, they brought
in an ethnic German baker. But he couldn't bake nearly
as well as Rosenstajn. Rosenstajn had had two thousand
years of practice, remarked Jascha. So they brought him
back, gave him a special permit and ordered him to
start baking. He was allowed to live in a tiny unheated
storage space behind the shop. But he missed his wife.

She looked out the window at the falling snow whipped by a gust of Russian wind. He used to visit her and come out through the tunnel on Ogrodowa Street. I know this, said Jascha. It was the Accountant who arranged it. He knew Rosenstajn from the former life. And do you know what happened? asked Lilka. Yes I do, replied Jascha. We knew everything that went on in the ghetto. We couldn't have done business if we didn't.

My mother didn't want me involved with you, said Lilka suddenly. She referred to you as "that smuggler of yours." What else was I? he asked. Although she didn't mind asking me to "organize" things from The Other Side when it suited her.

Lilka pulled closed her woolen robe. You never liked her. No, he agreed, I never did. She was a beauty, said Lilka. With her pale blonde hair and big blue eyes. Everyone said so. Men were enchanted with her. Not this one, he said. Even in those days what she did was not permissible. She was trying to survive, said Lilka. How did that make her different from anyone else? he wanted to know.

Once your mother asked me to organize a silk umbrella from The Other Side. I thought she was joking. To twirl as she made her way among the corpses? She was used to a certain kind of life, said Lilka. And the rest of us? he asked. Had we come from nowhere?

Jascha poured out more coffee. It happened on a Tuesday that Rosenstajn left us for a better world. They had let some "tourists" in. Officers and their girlfriends, friends of Hans Frank, come there to amuse themselves, to gape at the dying Jews in the zoo of the ghetto. I heard the women, wives of officers, complaining in high-pitched voices. What a stench, they cried. Don't they ever wash? How dirty they are, the Jews. And the children. They don't even dress properly, they're missing teeth. Is this the way Jews take care of their children? And all of them beggars. Disgusting.

What savages they are, these Jews. You wouldn't see German children behaving this way. Sometimes the tourists were given whips and guns to amuse themselves with. Another Jew lashed or shot? What difference? They were all going to disappear anyway.

As the tourists walked through the filthy streets, everyone fled at their approach. A man with a rotting blanket wrapped around him, barefoot in the winter snow, tried to get away from Them. But he could no longer walk. He didn't look at Them. It was death to look at one of Them. His cheekbones protruded, his eyes were milky with death. One of the women with a breathless shriek flung a coin at the man. But he was too weak to pick it up.

Lilka sat rigid, her eyes on the tablecloth. She ran a finger over a lump in the white linen spread. Look at that, she said, it's been darned. She clicked her tongue. So shabby. What else should it be? he asked. Has anyone prospered under the Communists? She lit a cigarette and stared out the window.

Rosenstajn was walking down Leszno Street, Jascha said. Suddenly he was grabbed by a German policeman who ordered him to run. Who knows why they chose him. What could he do? The street had emptied out in a hurry. The policemen wished the tourists happy hunting. Rosenstajn ran, zigzagging. But it did him no good. He was the only one, a perfect target. They shot at him as he ran. What a good time they had. The Accountant heard about it and sent a man to stop it. But it was too late. That was the end of Rosenstajn's baking. The SS who patronized the place were very annoyed. They shot two Jewish policemen. What did they have to do with it? asked Lilka. Nothing at all, replied Jascha.

Lilka put down her roll and wiped her fingers. I can't eat anymore, she said. I've lost my appetite. Give it to me, said Jascha, holding out his hand. I'm ravenous. I could eat a dozen rolls, one right after the other.

Lilka sat motionless. November 1940, she said. The gates were closing on the Jews. Do you remember, Jascha? My mother didn't want to move. Move to northern

Warsaw? she asked. Is that where they're planning to put us? The place is a slum. But the world had changed. And my mother no longer occupied the same place in it. Ha, cried Jascha. Did anyone want to move? Why is your mother always an exception?

My mother put on her hat and gloves. I'm going to headquarters, she said. When had her beauty ever failed her? I pleaded with her not to go. Mama, I cried, people go in there and they don't come out. She patted my cheek cooly. I'll be back, she told me. Mama, I said, you're out of your mind. Why take such a risk? When Papa went out, he didn't come back. Don't mention your father, she said sharply. Jascha read the paper.

How wrong you were, Lilka, she said when she returned. I met a very nice man. An officer. Very courteous. He complimented me on my German. He has promised to find us a nice apartment in the Jewish Quarter. They were not yet calling it the ghetto. Mama! I cried. My mother shook her head. She had gotten harder since my father disappeared. My innocent little flower, she said mockingly. She pulled off her gloves. Do you know what he said to me? Surely, my dear Frau Reifmann, you are not Jewish. I can't hear this, said Jascha. She did what she could, replied Lilka. Enough, Lilka. Don't provoke me.

True to his word, my mother's new friend found us an apartment on Sienna Street. The street they called The Champs-Élysées of the ghetto, said Jascha. Right up against The Other Side. Would you have rather we lived in a hole in the ground on Nalewki Street? she asked. No, darling, I'm just mentioning it.

Lilka blotted her mouth with her napkin. The night before we moved to the ghetto, we had a visit from the concierge, Pani Kowalska. She climbed up the stairs, wheezing at every step. She was short and dumpy and her skin had a yellowish cast. One eye bulged from her head. She appeared in a faded housedress, several layers of woolen cardigans and the scuffed slippers she always wore. Breathing heavily, her face flushed, she held out a shapeless swollen hand. Pani Reifmann, she said, give me your jewels. She smiled slyly. Better I should have them than the Others. Give them to me, she said softly. Where you're going, you won't be needing them. That time, my mother closed the door in her face. The next night she was back with "her cousin," who carried a truncheon in his hand.

And this, said Jascha, turning a page, is the Warsaw you were so anxious to return to.

Two days later, said Lilka, the movers began to pack up what had not been confiscated. And then suddenly they stopped. They sat down, surly, smoking. That's enough, they said. We're finished. My mother was in another room. Mama, they don't want to work anymore. What? she cried. Who do they think they are? But the world had changed. And people like my mother no longer held the reins of power. She went in to them, in her elegant suit, her French shoes, with her blonde hair. What is the meaning of this? she asked them. For a moment they were in awe of her. And then they remembered she was only a Jew.

We're not working until we get paid more. But we agreed on the price, said my mother. One small wiry mover stood looking at her, a cigarette hanging from his lip. We've changed our mind. It can happen to anyone, he added. The others smiled. My mother was not yet used to the new order. She stared at them in disbelief. And then she pulled herself together. She offered them this many *zloty* and not a penny more. Take it or leave it. Otherwise, she said, she'd get someone else. You don't have much time, one of them ventured. They'll be closing the gates. And if you're not inside . . . He made a motion across his throat.

That night as we sat among the boxes, Marysia came in, drying her eyes with a corner of her apron. Her thin hair was pulled back with clear plastic combs, and I could see her long creased earlobes that I used to tug on when I was a child. It will soon be over, she said. And you'll be back.

We stepped into the *droshky* my mother had hired on November 13th of '40, two days before they closed the gates. We had one suitcase each. The rest was going by wagon to Sienna Street. Never have you seen such chaos. The streets were packed with people pushing handcarts piled high with furniture and bedding, mattresses, wardrobes, pots and pans. A whole life lashed to the back of a wagon. In their panic they collided; armoires and beds tumbled from their moorings and crashed onto the pavement.

Horses reared; we were nearly struck by falling furniture. The porters had more than they could handle. People shrieked, cried out. An unspeakable din. The Jews were being cheated right and left. Just before they closed the gates, the panic was indescribable. The Jews were forbidden to remove anything from their apartments. Yet somehow the streets were full of carts hauling Jewish furniture.

Small children were pressed into the bedding. They tumbled around, holding on, shouting out as the cart careened around a corner. Sometimes a badly balanced load fell over, sometimes a cart overturned. One wagon drawn by a skittish horse took off over the cobblestones and disappeared. The driver had lost control. Those who had households full of nice furniture, paintings, silver, Oriental rugs, gave up their lives. So did everyone else.

A child ran after his family's wagon. In the turmoil he had been left behind. At last the wagon was turned around and they came back for him. Sitting on the curb he refused to come. No, he cried, I want to live on my own. Soon he would. What chaos. The shrieking, the cries, the horses were driven nearly mad by the human hysteria. And over the cobblestone streets hung a bright November sky, the round disc of the sun shining in the blue skies.

The drivers were charging a fortune. And those who had traded apartments with the Jews were cleaning up. Some of them stripped the apartments of everything that made them habitable and then turned them over. Others moved into the Jews' apartments and then sold theirs again to someone else. There was no recourse to the law. There was no longer any law for the Jews. And then They came out and began to beat the Jews with truncheons. They tugged at Jewish beards until they had torn them out. A horse who had made the mistake of pressing his flank against one of Them was beaten to death . . . Lilka stopped, exhausted.

At last we walked up the stairs to our new apartment and waited for the wagon with our furniture to arrive. We're still waiting, said Lilka. That first night in the ghetto we slept on the floor. Papa, I whispered, come and rescue us. But he was not coming back. We were on our own. Shut up behind six foot walls. And everything that belonged to us left behind.

Out the window the snow flew around as though pursued by furies. What madness, he said, licking his finger and turning the page of the newspaper. Go back? Didn't we have enough of it Back There? She smoked one of her blond cigarettes, blowing the smoke out in a thin plume. Why have we come? Why indeed? he replied.

I'm going to cancel, she said. Do it now, he told her. She tied her bathrobe and went to the phone. We ordered a car, she said. He's already here? Well would you tell him that there's been a change of plans. We will not be going to the ghetto after all. No, not at all. Thank you. She hung up the phone. He told me that I speak good Polish. She sat down abruptly. What's the matter with me? My heart is pounding, I feel short of breath. Can it be, he asked, that you've forgotten what fear is?

She watched the snow falling. I remember the winter of 1940, she said. We were cold all the time. They had closed the gates and we couldn't get out. The snow fell and already people began to die. It didn't take long. 186 calories a day. Do you remember, Jascha? Those were the rations for a Jew. Sometimes it snowed for days without stopping. The cold entered into your bones. You felt that your eyes would freeze in their sockets. Polish winter, he said. When was it ever different? When God in His wisdom froze Poland, He should have frozen all the Poles along with it. How wicked you are, she said. Not wicked enough, he replied.

Lilka ate a sweet roll. All over the ghetto, the pipes froze. The whole place became a giant dunghill. In the midst of all that, my mother had managed to bring her fur coat. She wore it with a stylish hat. Until the Jews were ordered to give up every shred of fur they possessed. On pain of death. Every fur coat, fur collar, fur cuff had to go. You could spot a Jew by a coat with the collar removed. No one had warm coats any longer. Then the Poles arrived, looking for furs at fire-sale prices. My mother sold hers for a fraction of what it was worth. The mink coat my father had given her when I was born.

Lilka heaped sugar into her cold coffee. I imagined the German soldiers on the Eastern front in long mink coats with generous collars. Oh darling, said Jascha. Don't be silly. They remade them. They didn't want their soldiers looking like old Jewish ladies, did they? Bad for morale.

Lilka took up her white napkin and dabbed at her mouth. My parents used to stroll together arm in arm, she said. How elegant they looked. She in her black velvet hat with the veil that he had bought for her in Paris, he in his beautifully cut navy blue suits and silk ties. But one day my father could no longer go out.

My mother told me to read to him, play the piano, recite Mickiewicz poems to him. She played cards with him, brought him newspapers and books. He couldn't bear being cooped up in the house. He was restless all the time, drumming his fingers on his desk, smoking endless cigarettes. One day he decided to go out. With your looks, said my mother, it's impossible. A short walk, he told her, and then I'll be back. I want to see what's happening out in the world. I'll lose my mind if I don't get some fresh air. And he held up the false papers he had paid so much for. I remember he was wearing his soft camel's hair coat, his dark hair combed back. She tried to hold him back, clutching at his lapels, pleading with him not to go. Lilka, she said, help me. But how could we stop him? He was determined. And telling her not to worry, that he'd be back in a moment, he kissed her and went . . .

She pressed out her cigarette in a saucer and lit another
one. For years I used to think that if I went back to
Warsaw I would find him. There had been a mix-up.
He had been taken away, but he had survived. He had
come back and was looking for us. If I could only get
back to Warsaw, there he would be . . . He sighed. My
darling, he said wearily, do you think you are the only
one? Everyone dreamed these dreams.

After that my mother became tougher, harder.
Wasn't she always that? asked Jascha. Beneath the
French perfume and the pearls? What do you know
about the way she was? asked Lilka. She was the one
who arranged for me to be a nurse-in-training at the
hospital, who got me my "ticket to life." At that time,
They still wanted to give the illusion that only the
healthy were being shipped off to work in the East.
Hospital personnel were still exempt from deporta-
tion. He studied the newspaper. And she managed
to smuggle money into the ghetto so we could eat.
She had never cooked, we always had a cook. Now
in the midst of the crowds and the filth she was out

on the street every day organizing food with the rest of them. Well well, said Jascha. Good for her. He turned the page. She glared at him. There's nothing I can say about her without you making some negative remark. What she did was unacceptable, he said. Since when are you the moral arbiter of the ghetto? she cried.

She stuffed a chunk of bread into her mouth. Do you know everything? Do you understand everything? she cried. You don't. The white marble clock on the mantel was ticking. A woman in white marble held the round enamel clock face in her arms. Does she never get tired? asked Jascha. Who? demanded Lilka. He pointed to the clock. She shook her head. What an irritating man you are. He looked at her from under heavy-lidded eyes. Your mother went out once a week by the Grzybowska Gate to meet her German officer. How do you know that? cried Lilka. Did the Accountant not know everything? He put out a hand to her. That's enough for now, darling. No, she said fiercely and pushed his hand away. Don't give me your hand.

He shook his head. Why are we fighting? It was so long ago. Lilka spread a roll with black jam. Not to me, she said. It's as near to me as last week.

Come and sit on my lap, he said. Nothing is the way it was. Let me tickle you and whisper in your ear. Don't be so silly, she said and poured out more coffee. He grinned. Come on, darling. Don't be shy. She shook her head. You're crazy. He laughed. This is what you used to do. Pretend to be a shy virgin. You did it on purpose because you knew how it excited me. Did it? she asked. I remember times when I wasn't a shy virgin at all. She lifted her neck seductively. Or have you forgotten that? He stared at her. Your mother had that same gesture. Don't talk to me, said Lilka.

The snow had piled up on the windowsill, obscuring the bottom part of the window. Look at that, said Lilka. Soon we'll be snowed in entirely. Good, he replied. Then we won't have to tramp the streets of Warsaw like homeless Jews. Why homeless Jews? she asked in surprise. Aren't we? he asked.

Jascha stood up from the breakfast table, stubbed out his cigarette and began to strip off his clothes. Lilka looked at him in astonishment. Have you gone insane? she asked. He dropped his clothes on the carpet and went into the bathroom. I'm taking a hot bath, he announced. In lieu of a trip to the ghetto.

He turned on the taps all the way. A narrow stream of rusty water issued forth. What is this? he cried. Do they call this trickle running water? He placed his open palm beneath the faucet. And it's lukewarm, he reported. Come in, darling, he said. All is forgiven. She stood in the doorway. This is Poland now, she said. Everything was better before the war. Then we had hot water. Not in the ghetto, he said. I'm not talking about the ghetto, she said. I'm talking about before.

The taps snorted and choked and pressed out hot water in spurts. But soon steam rose up from the water and he turned to her with a smile. Get in, he said. Before it changes its mind. Let us steam ourselves like in a

Russian bathhouse. Let us switch each other with birch branches and talk about Eternity.

He lay stretched out in the old veined marble tub, his broad shoulders resting against the stone, the water up to his neck. He closed his eyes. Ah, how delicious. I could stay in here forever. Come in, darling. Get yourself clean. The steam rose up off the water. Jascha, she said, your hair is getting all curly with the steam. She reached down a hand to touch his hair. I remember your dark curls, she said softly. That was long ago, he replied.

She sat down on the edge of the tub and lit a cigarette. I remember your dark eyes. How handsome you were in your high leather boots. When I first saw you, I thought you were a Jewish policeman. In the ghetto, they were the only Jews with boots like that. And you were as cocky as they were. But you weren't wearing their special yellow armband. Only a blue and white one with a star. Like the rest of us. He's an informer, I thought. Whatever he is, it isn't good. He laughed now. What

was good, in your opinion? A scholar who would soon
be dead? A lawyer when nothing was any longer legal?
He shook his head. What a silly girl.

One morning, he said, I was walking down Karmelicka,
on my way to see the Accountant. It had snowed during
the night. Already the snow on the ground had been
stamped down by passersby, by carts, by rickshaws.
Along the road men in long dark coats, with rags tied
around their shoes and armbands on their sleeves, were
shoveling snow, their faces blue with cold. What else
was new? This was not what caught my eye.

What caught my eye was a procession walking two
abreast down the crowded street. Girls dressed in
immaculate pink and white striped uniforms. Nurses-
in-training with white aprons and navy blue woolen
capes with red linings. And on their heads starched
white caps. Freshly scrubbed, well fed. Nothing looked
that clean in the ghetto. They looked like angels in the
midst of all that filth. Like a vision. I was in love with
them all.

But it was you I had my eye on. What a walk you had.
The way you moved. I have to have her, I said to myself.
I walked alongside you until at last you turned to look
at me. I got a shock. At first I thought there must be
some mistake: those bright blue eyes, that flaxen hair,
those high cheekbones. What a beauty you were. This
girl is Polish, I said to myself, she "looks good" as we
said Back There. What is she doing in here? But then
you turned toward me. And I saw the expression in
your eyes. I knew right away. I could always tell.

How insistent you were, she said now. Where did
you get that flaxen hair, darling? you asked me. I was
appalled. Is this the way young men in the ghetto
behave now? I asked you. No manners at all. You
shrugged. The Germans have confiscated our etiquette
books, you said. Have you forgotten where you are? I
didn't want to have anything to do with you, said Lilka.
What a liar, he said.

He dipped the washcloth in the water. Where did you
get that flaxen hair? Jewish mothers buy flaxen hair like

that in the marketplace for their dark-haired daughters. No one wanted our dark stubborn curls. They couldn't wait to get rid of them . . . That's what you said Back There, said Lilka. And then what did I say? he asked now. You said that you wanted me for your own. He nodded. At least she remembers something.

When you walked away, said Lilka, Magda said to me: that's Jascha Krasniewski. He's one of the biggest smugglers in the ghetto. He has a thousand girlfriends. A slight exaggeration, he said. He smiled. But not by much.

I thought about you all the time, he said. I wanted to lie down in your flaxen hair. I wanted to take you to bed right away. I wanted you to belong to me completely. What didn't I want? The Accountant saw the state I was in and told me to be careful. He told me that mooning around on the job could be disastrous. Jascha reached out a wet hand to her. You were madly in love with me. I wasn't, she replied. You're soaking me, she cried. He

grinned. What a terrible liar you are. She smiled slowly
and dried her hand on the towel. Maybe I am.

She pulled the puckered paper wrapper from a bar of
dark green soap and handed it to him. He held it up to
his nose and closed his eyes. Pine, he said. He inhaled
again. It smells of the Praga forest. Do you know how
much this was worth Back Then? 50 *groszy*. Later it was
worth more. In January of '41 a piece of soap was 80
groszy. In October of '41 it was 1 *zloty* 60. And by Feb-
ruary of '42 only doctors, midwives, dentists, hospi-
tals, and the prison had the right to it. I still remember
every price on the black market, he said. Ask me the
day, the year, the merchandise, and I'll tell you. What
we would have given, she said, for a hot bath.

Do you remember that miserable ersatz fat they tried to
peddle as soap? he asked. The lather was useless. And
afterward a sticky paste stuck to your skin. I brought
in real soap. With real lather. With my soap you could
really get clean. She pressed a towel to her moist face.
What did it matter? she asked. The stench followed you

everywhere. The whole place stank to high heaven. The ghetto was a giant dunghill. What was another unwashed body? Those who could afford to pay for real soap were the lucky ones, he said. They felt human. Not like those stinking beggars who hadn't washed in months. He spat. Jascha, she said. How can you be like that?

He slid under the water and came up snorting, blowing out water and slicking back his hair. Water dripped from his cheeks and eyelids. Why should I go back to the ghetto? Do I not know every street, every gate, every blackened building like the back of my hand? There are twenty-three gates and I know every one of them. Every open drain, every sewer, every tunnel that leads to The Other Side. I know which buildings are riddled with holes and passageways like Swiss cheese. I know where they have drilled through the walls of an apartment on Our Side to one on The Other Side. Do I not know where they have loosened the bricks in the Wall? So we can remove them once the guards have been paid off?

Do I not know every Jewish policeman, every guard and his schedule. Until, that is, they brought in the Ukrainians and I had to start all over again. Do I not know where the rubber tube leads from a window on The Other Side to a window on Our Side for milk to run through and collect in buckets on the other end? Do I not know every inch of the cemetery? Where the hearses once returned from the cemetery stuffed with black-market merchandise, until there were too many dead and they had to throw them into pits. My darling, I know the ghetto like the back of my hand. I was, you might say, a master topographer. You had to be in those days. Without that I would have been another corpse on Pinkiert's wagon. He took up the dripping washcloth and handed it to her. Go back? What for? He put a finger to his forehead. The entire ghetto is in here.

He laid his head back against the marble rim of the tub. We took our orders from the Accountant. King of the Smugglers. In the ghetto only Gancwajch and his Thirteen who were in the pocket of the Gestapo did more smuggling business. In a small basement room where the walls breathed out moisture and rot, the Accountant sat behind a shabby desk, lifted from a deserted Jewish apartment. The top of his desk was nearly empty. There were only boxes of smuggled cigarettes which he smoked one after the other, and a small creased photo of his twin girls who were six.

His eyes, behind thick lenses, were magnified until they looked like the eyes of a cow. But there was nothing bovine about the expression in them. His gaze was hard and unrelenting. He wrote nothing down. He kept it all in his head. Schedules, prices, personnel. He could remember endless lists of figures. The prices of black-market goods changed every hour in the ghetto and the Accountant forgot nothing. A real Jewish brain, added Jascha.

I must know everything that's happening at every moment, the Accountant said to me. What's happening on Our Side, what's happening on The Other Side.

What's coming in, what's going out, who's on guard, where the next roundup will take place. I need contacts and informants everywhere. My payroll, he said, includes every kind of scum. Never mind. I need information however I can get it.

Somewhere up above, he told me, there is an Accountant keeping track of everything that goes on here on Earth. Beside Him I am more insignificant than a mayfly. But in this little quarter of the woods, this appalling little section of the globe, I know everything. Nothing escapes my notice.

The Accountant liked me, said Jascha. And one day, when I had been working for him for three months, he gave me an important assignment.

Jascha turned on the hot water tap. The water's getting cold, he said. How long are you planning to stay in there? she asked. He lay back. The water covered his chest and lapped at his neck. Forever, he replied.

Jascha closed his eyes. The moon was rising over the darkened streets of the ghetto, he said. Overhead the night sky was sprinkled with stars. As cold and dead as Their eyes. Well well, I thought, the moon will rise as it has risen for thousands of years and turn its glowing face to the ghetto. What does it care what happens here on Earth? We had gone back to a distant century where there was no light at night but the dim light from the small fires set at the sentry posts against the Wall. As the inhabitants packed eight to a room groaned in their sleep, I would be heading for the cemetery. Not in a casket or thrown onto a wagon heaped with corpses. I would be walking there on my own two legs.

I walked through the silent streets, dark as a medieval village. The streets were black with filth and rubbish, the stench was overwhelming. On the sidewalks, covered in sheets of newspaper, lay bodies who would never see the stars again. I barely saw them. I was immune to them by then. There in the shadow of a half ruined building lay a small child caterwauling like a cat for something to eat. I reached into my pocket and threw him a piece of bread. There was no electricity—no light and no heat. And walls all around. I knew my way in the dark. I knew every street, every building, every tunnel, every sewer, every crossing. I walked quickly. I had a rendezvous in the Jewish cemetery.

She took the washcloth from him. Lean forward, she said, and she began to soap his back. You'll need a haircut soon, it's curling over your neck. All right, that's enough, he said and slid down until the water was at his neck and his head rested against the marble rim of the tub.

At the corner of Gęsia and Okopowa, Avi and Stasik and Jurek joined me. Jurek was nervous, as always, his head twisting on his thin neck. If they don't come? he asked. If they change the guards on us? If the trucks aren't there? Jurek, I said to him, in this world of ours anything can happen. And does. I shouldn't have agreed to come along, he muttered.

Why? I asked him. Because you risk your life? So what? Even if you do nothing, you risk it. What's the difference? Six of one, half a dozen of the other.

We passed through the large brick gates of the cemetery. Shards of moonlight fell on the Hebrew lettering of the old stones. The open pits were filled with corpses, waiting for the new arrivals that would surely come. We passed over the uneven ground, careful not to fall in with the rest. And made our way to the Wall we shared with Powązki, the Catholic cemetery. Half the black market operated over that shared Wall.

It was 10:15 at night. We had agreed on a 10:30 delivery. We were smoking and Jurek once again speaks up. What if they don't come? Stasik says to him: if they don't, they don't. What shall we do? Complain to Berlin? He was driving us crazy, that Jurek.

It was 10:40 when we heard a whistle from the Polish cemetery on the other side of the Wall. All the guards had been paid off. But only the ones on that shift. We had half an hour before the guards changed. It took four of us to set up our wooden ramp, leaning it against the ancient wall. We could hear the sound of their ramp going up, the sound of voices. And then we heard a truck door opening and the lowing of cattle. Well, I said, they're here. And there beneath the light of the moon, twenty-six farting, shitting cows made their way up the Christian ramp and came down the other side on the Jewish ramp. What a deafening noise of hooves. They moaned, they grunted and groaned.

What a sight as they stood framed in the moonlight on their way down. Even Jurek smiled. When the first one came off the ramp Stasik slapped her on the rump. Where's your armband? he growled. Twenty-five cows came over. Then what happens? The twenty-sixth balked. She didn't want to come into the ghetto. Can you blame her? We could hear them swearing in Polish, calling her every name in the book. She wouldn't come.

What a clever cow. They shouted at her, they gave her precious sugar, they did everything but climb on her back. At last I gave a whistle. I was afraid the guards would change. Let it be, I called out. You keep her. But remember, you owe us one. They threw a few packets of cigarettes over the Wall. Shalom, Jewish goniffs, they called out with a laugh. Never mind. We had the cows.

Now we tried to load them onto the trucks. One wandered off and almost fell into one of the open pits. Another started to go back up the ramp. Do I look like a cowherd? What chaos. As we prodded them into the truck, these Aryan cows, I thought, just like the Jews, once in the ghetto you won't get out again. Suddenly I was sorry for them. They too had mothers and fathers, sisters and grandmothers, uncles and aunts.

I rode in back with the cows. Stasik went home. Avi and Jurek sat up front next to the driver. The cows were packed in so tightly they couldn't move. Well, Aryan cows, I said to them. How does it feel to be in the ghetto? Packed together in trucks. Like sardines. Like Jews. They groaned and mooed, their soft mouths wet with slobber. I gathered they weren't too happy to be on the Jewish side. The truck slowed, and in their panic they began to push against each other and against me. I felt squeezed in by warm flanks, and I slapped them and pushed them aside.

The truck entered a courtyard where there was a warehouse. The driver got out and knocked four times and the door was rolled up. We drove downhill and soon came to a halt. The back door opened. We were below ground in a large empty warehouse. There were signs of the previous occupants—cow patties, flattened hay, feeding troughs. Here, underground, men in overalls led the cows down one by one from the truck.

Where are their armbands? cried one. We won't take them without. I looked around me in amazement. I hadn't seen anything like this before. A small emaciated man with tiny black eyes watched me. We milk some of them, we slaughter the rest. Come back tomorrow for some milk. The Accountant has promised a pail of it to a Polish policeman with young children who gives him information.

It was a primitive structure. It looked like a great barn from the previous century. Now it housed twenty-five cows. With relief I took out a cigarette and lit it. Put that out, cried the little man, are you crazy? With all the straw in here and no exit. Do you want twenty-six cows to go up in smoke and me along with them? I put it out and placed it back in my pocket. Twenty-five, I corrected him. The twenty-sixth didn't want to come. I'm wondering, I said, how the hell I get out of here. The man grinned. Take the stairs, he said and pointed to the back. It was two flights up. When I was back on street level, I had to go through several doors until I was shown a small doorway. I knocked twice and went through to an apartment.

A large woman with swollen legs sat knitting in a rocking chair. She asked my name and holding her knitting in one hand, checked me off on a list. Have you got cigarettes for me? she asked and held out her hand. I gave her a few packs along with what we owed her. How many tonight? she wanted to know. Twenty-five, I told her. The twenty-sixth refused to come into the ghetto. Smart cow, she said. Everyone seemed to share that sentiment. The price of milk will go down tomorrow, she said. It's always that way. She went back to her knitting. Don't take Karmelicka Street tonight, she said. They've brought in some tourists.

They shot Avi and Jurek on their way home, he said. A lunar moth lives eight days. The average lifespan of a Jew in those days. He lay back and closed his eyes. I've forgotten nothing.

Lilka lifted the carefully folded white bath towel. It's time to get out, she said. You've been in there for ages. Are we in such a hurry? he wanted to know. I remember the first time, said Lilka. She touched his wet curls. You said to me: what are you waiting for? Do you think we live forever? Do you think this parade goes on and on? The days in the ghetto are short and the nights shorter. From one moment to the next you can disappear. So you don't take years to make up your mind. These days a long engagement has lost all meaning, you said. The bride to be could be dead in twenty-four hours. But, said Lilka, I wasn't sure . . . Ha, replied Jascha, splashing his neck. As though I had to talk you into it.

That long ago night in his tiny room in the ghetto, she had rolled toward him and pressed herself against him on the tattered blanket. Here we are in the Garden of Eden, he said. She took one of his dark curls between her fingers. Tell me, she said, what was it like, the Garden of Eden? Ha, he replied. What was it not like? Full of every tree and flower in creation, fruits hung from the trees in their fullness, eternally ripe. Birds sang, butterflies also sang. What happiness. Morning, evening, another day. Time without end. And then Adam extracted a rib and brought forth his misfortune. She pinched him. How can you say such a thing? He gripped her arm. Come here my sweetheart, let me touch your skin, smoother and sweeter than any pear or peach that hung in the garden. Come my angel.

Tell me more, she said, about the Garden of Eden. Why did Adam listen to her? he asked, his hand between her legs. What a madman. She comes up with a crazy scheme and he falls for it. Their skin glistened with moisture, her hair was wet at the temples. She pressed her face into his cheek. Where did they do it? she asked. Where did they do it? They did it everywhere.

The garden was theirs. Adam lay with her on soft ground, open to the sky. He didn't yet know that God saw it all. Did they do everything together? she wanted to know. Everything, he replied. Everything there was to do in this situation. Show me, she whispered. Show me what he did to her in the heat of the day. He took a handful of her damp hair and kissed her mouth. He ran his hand along the curve of her waist. And then he climbed on top of her. I'll show you, he said. I'll show you what they did. Again and again. Until the snake came . . .

It was stifling in that little room, she said now. No air, no light. She dried her hands. But that night we forgot, didn't we, where we were? I was madly in love with

you, he said. But I didn't want to show it. It's not good
to spoil women. They shouldn't know their power over
you. Do you think I couldn't tell? she asked. When we
marched to the hospital the next morning, I was in a
daze. God forgive me, I didn't see the dead and dying,
I even forgot the terrible stench.

Have you been with your smuggler? my mother asked
with disdain, and she turned away. What a foolish girl
you are. Lilka shrugged. She wanted a Jewish policeman for me. Not a smuggler. The bitch, said Jascha. She
understood nothing. Jascha! You mustn't talk about her
that way.

The bathroom was filled with steam. It fogged the mirror and floated above the tub and the sink. I can barely
see, said Lilka, mopping off her face. It's like a steam
bath in here. An old Jewish tradition, he remarked.

In the ghetto, said Lilka, you couldn't survive if you
didn't have someone to love. It was the only thing

that could save you from despair. Everyone was getting together—old women with younger men, old men with young girls, scholars with former party girls, yeshiva boys with modern girls.

Before the war, said Jascha, two doors away from us was a pharmacy with a hunchbacked woman behind the counter. She was a famous matchmaker. Nearly invisible in the dim recesses of that little shop, she dispensed all kinds of medicine while sizing up her customers. She spoke in a small voice like a bird. Because of her hump she could not look up at customers directly, but had to incline her head slightly. She could read people in a moment. She cross-pollinated the shy with the bold, the plain with the dazzling. She saw something that others did not. It will work very well, she would say whenever her taste was questioned. Let the lion lie down with the lamb, the dove with the coyote, the rabbit with the hawk. You'll see. Golda knows.

Would she have matched us, I wonder? Lilka wanted to know. Never, he replied. You're not my type. And seeing her expression he stroked her cheek. Oh darling, I'm only joking. You're still a beauty, he told her. I'm nearly sixty. Not to me, he replied. For me you're still a young girl.

She reached over and touched his chest. What's all this? he asked. I was afraid, she said softly. We were all afraid, he replied. I mean of you. With your strong arms and fierce dark eyes. I was only sixteen. You were twenty-three. I had kissed a few boys, nothing more. You were a man of the world. Of a small enclosed world, he replied, where everyone was about to die.

They needed the Poles to point out the Jews to Them, said Lilka. If they didn't have hair and eyes as black as night, They couldn't pick them out. She smiled. Except for you, my angel. With those dark curls and dark eyes. The water splashed as he sat up in the tub. I don't look Jewish, he protested. No? she asked. Not at all, he said hotly.

She ground out her cigarette and stood up. She unfurled the white towel and held it up for him. He stood up and cockily pressed out his chest. She looked at his strong arms and chest, his muscular legs. You're still handsome, she told him. I always was, he replied. And conceited, she added. You were always that, too. Not at all, darling, he said. I only pretended. And only with my own. How conceited, he asked, could a Jew in the ghetto be? The life of the handsomest, smartest Jew hung by a thread. She wrapped him in the towel. He pulled her against him. Come to bed. We'll go back to the beginning.

He went into the room and lay down on the bed and pulled the eiderdown over him. Come darling, he said, lie down beside me. Don't leave me alone in the city of Warsaw that is no more. She lay down beside him beneath the eiderdown. Like a law abiding Jewish couple, he said, and took her hand.

Late one night in the ghetto, she said, when we had already gone to bed, the doorbell rang. My mother crept to the door in the darkness. Through the door we heard someone whisper in Yiddish: It is I. My mother opened the door a crack. I stood behind her. My mother gave a small cry. There stood a ghost. His gray hair and sidelocks hung in wisps, his black caftan fell in tattered folds from his bony shoulders. His skin had a bluish tinge, his eyes were rimmed in red. One side of his forehead was discolored by a large purplish bruise. Dear God in Heaven, said my mother. It only needed this.

Grandfather, I cried out. It was my father's father. How thin he was, his bones like a bird's. He collapsed into a chair. I went to the kitchen and brought him water and bread and some marmalade. My mother watched him with a frown. Father, she said, how in the world did you get here? All the way from Lodz?

What bearded Jew in a long gabardine could survive? The black gabardines, the beards, the sidelocks of pious Jews drove Them into a frenzy. God looks after us, said my grandfather. My mother laughed mirthlessly. Here?

In the ghetto? Now Grandfather reached underneath his caftan and drew out a small prayer book. I must recite the prayer for a safe arrival after a long journey. My mother groaned. Father, she pleaded. This is not a House of Prayer.

When he had eaten, my mother turned to me. Tell him, Lilka, she whispered. My grandfather placed his finger on the page of his prayer book. No need, he said. Three months ago my son appeared to me in a dream, wrapped in a shroud. That is when he disappeared, said my mother in surprise. Yes, replied Grandfather, in August. The month he was born. He bent his head and began to pray. My mother shook her head. When she had left the room, my grandfather put his hand on my arm. Everyone is trying to survive, he said to me. She too.

One day, said Lilka, I had to go to Nalewki on an errand for Grandfather. Nalewki was one of the worst. They were all the worst, said Jascha. We wouldn't let him leave the house. Not with his beard, his black hat, his gabardine. I offered to buy him Polish clothes at the market.

Grandfather, I pleaded with him, shave off your beard. You know what happens to Them when they see a Jewish beard. They go even crazier. He pinched my cheek. Shave off my beard? he said. And then who would I be? God wouldn't recognize me without my beard. And my eyes? What shall I do with my eyes? Grandfather, I said sharply, for God's sake be practical. He looked at me sadly. Practical, my darling? Is that how we will survive?

I went to the man who sold old Hebrew books out of a broken down baby carriage on Nalewki Street. He always had plenty of browsers. Whether they bought or not I don't know. People stole the books and ran off down the street. He was an old man and couldn't pursue them. So he hired a young boy, he couldn't have been more than six, to run after the thieves. I remember that boy. He had black eyes like olives and had lost all his teeth. But he could run, and panting, he would bring back a volume and the bookseller would give him a coin. How could the man make a profit? He was paying more to get back what was stolen.

The bookseller would give me a small list of volumes he thought would interest my grandfather. I would get money from my mother on some pretext or other and buy them for him. My grandfather kept them stacked up beside his mattress, old black books with Hebrew lettering in fading gilt.

Shall I teach you Hebrew? my grandfather asked me when he saw me looking. I shook my head. I wouldn't have the patience. If you dip into these works, he told me, you forget the outer world. I can't, Grandfather, I said. It's the only way, he said. Otherwise how can one live?

Sometimes we sat side by side and a strange calm was transmitted to me. He stroked his beard slowly and sometimes he recited a psalm. His skin was like

parchment, his long fingers were bony and white. His
red rimmed eyes were always calm. He's somewhere
else, my mother would say irritably. He's not of this
world. Why must you treat him this way? I would ask
her. He's father's father. Luckily your father was nothing like him, she said. Why didn't he stay in Lodz? she
asked. Why must he complicate everything?

I went into our secret hiding places and showed Grandfather our packets of sugar, sausage, even tea. He
looked at me in surprise. It's her smuggler, said my
mother. A low type. In these times, even that is per-
mitted, said Grandfather. Is that what it says in your
books? asked my mother. What she was up to, said Jascha, made smuggling look like a fairy story. All right,
all right, replied Lilka. Let's not get into all that.

He drove my mother crazy. Dear God in Heaven, she
said. Can one look more Jewish? That he arrived from
Lodz is a miracle equal to the parting of the Red Sea.
She was speaking like my father!

With Grandfather there the atmosphere in the apartment grew calmer. Neighbors came to see him. He makes me feel calmer, they said. A real *tsaddik*. Even my mother was softening toward him. I sometimes thought of my father, his son, who bought his suits in Paris, ordered his shoes from the finest boot maker in London. Who traveled to the capitals of Europe and never observed the Sabbath. Not long before my father was born, they had allowed the Jews to leave their shtetls. How quickly things had changed in one generation. The gates opened at last, said Jascha, and everyone rushed out. A few decades later they closed again. Your father was of the generation that could finally become European. Or so everyone thought. Gates open and close, he said. This time they closed forever.

There are no free miracles in this world, he observed. Not even from the Almighty. He turned in the soft bedding and reached for a cigarette. This miracle was paid for in hard cash. What do you mean? asked Lilka. The Accountant arranged it, said Jascha. He brought him in with another shipment from Lodz. We can squeeze one more in, he said. And this one, he added,

is as small as a bird. What do you mean? How did he
know about Grandfather? Jascha shrugged. I told him.
And you? How did you know? You told me you had
a grandfather you loved. I asked where he was. You
told me Lodz. I asked you his name. We had contacts
in the Lodz ghetto. We could find anyone. And for a
small fortune we could get him to Warsaw. I had made
money on a large shipment of kasha brought into the
ghetto. Take it, I told the Accountant and handed him
the cash. And let us bring her grandfather to her. Will
you find him in that swarming hive? he asked me. I
will find him, I replied. I had informers there, and I
told them to locate him and get him on a truck we had
coming back to Warsaw. Lilka stared at him. Why did
you never tell me? she asked.

The Accountant swore me to secrecy. But the Accountant has been gone for more than forty years, she said.
Why did you do it? Because I hated you. Because you
loved me. Because I loved you, he agreed. His beard
was soft as grass, said Lilka. He used to pull at it as
pious Jews do. You'll pull them out, I told him. He
would smile at me and pinch my cheek. Lilkele, he said

to me. Jews have been pulling at their beards since the world was created. They know how to do it so they don't lose a single hair.

She turned to Jascha beneath the soft eiderdown. My sweetheart, she murmured, and wound her fingers into his hair. Be careful, said Jascha, you'll pull them out. She laughed happily. Never has there been a more terrible man. She kissed his face and his mouth and the skin of his chest where his shirt was open. What else, she asked him, haven't you told me?

He took her hand in his. We spend our years like a sigh, my sweetheart. Like a watch of the night. She clicked her tongue. Don't be so morbid. You don't know the psalm? he asked her. You engulf men in sleep, at daybreak they are like grass that renews itself; at daybreak it flourishes anew . . . And then? he asked. What comes next? She shook her head. By dusk it withers and dries up. Didn't they teach you anything in that well-to-do household of yours? Where did you learn all this? she asked. Where? From the books the Jews left behind.

When they awoke, it was afternoon. Get up, cried Lilka, pressing his arm, we have to go out while there's still some light left. Otherwise how will we see what Warsaw has become? Is it strictly necessary? he asked. Please, Jascha, she pleaded. He turned over. Let me sleep, he said. I'm exhausted.

She lay smoking, looking out at the fading light. What an unbearable stench, she said. Every morning we walked down Karmelicka Street to the hospital. And passed through those streets of indescribable filth. Everywhere they cried out to us nurses to help them. Their dark eyes seemed fixed with fear and starvation. What could we do? There were hundreds more like them at the hospital, three to a bed, lying in the corridors so you could barely walk. They had been beaten nearly to death, they had typhus, they were dying of starvation. And what could we do for them? Almost nothing. The only medicine left was hundreds of boxes of suppositories. Suppositories? They were dying of dysentery.

They lay three to a bed, and bodies lay crowding the corridors so you could barely get through. There was nothing to cover them with. One little boy who was sick with typhus cried out: I want to steal. I want to kill. I want to eat. I want to be a German.

One evening as I was going home an ancient woman came up to me. She was tiny, skin and bones, covered in layers of rags. The skin was stretched tightly across her face and her eyes were large and expressionless. She reached out a kind of claw. From her throat came a weak croak and she said my name. I stared at her and could not understand how she knew me. The stench was terrible. It's Pani Rozen, she said hoarsely. I pulled back in disbelief. My old piano teacher. She had been pink and plump, with lively dark eyes and white teeth. Only a few years older than I. She was in love with Schubert. I've changed, she croaked sadly. She bent close to me and I forced myself not to recoil. I'm no longer human, she murmured.

Lilka, said Jascha, you mustn't think about this now. Another time. Only not now. What has come over me? she asked. I thought it was over. Beneath the eiderdown he took her in his arms. Come my baby, he said. It's all long ago. He stroked her hair. Only it's not, she said.

Do you remember the din? she asked him. The endless crying out and moaning, the screaming, the shouting, the singers on every corner singing their different songs, hoping to get a few pennies. No sooner were you out on the street than this unearthly clamor assaulted you. I remember a little boy of about six who used to stand on the corner of Pawia and Zamenhofa. I used to see him on the way to the hospital. He was so tiny he might have been four. His name was Avi. Dressed in rags, he sang old Yiddish songs—his mother had taught them to him and sent him out on the streets to get a few pennies. No one could resist him. Tiny and bird-like, he stood straight and immobile and opened his mouth wide like a bird and sang. He had a high clear voice. Soon everyone was weeping. Anyone who could manage put a coin in his hand.

While he sang, nearby his mother sold a few loaves of bread which she kept locked in a rabbit cage. Bread behind mesh bars so it wouldn't be stolen. She spoke courteously to buyers, calling them her dear customers and thanking them for their business. They would look at her in disbelief. This kind of behavior belonged to another life.

When he was finished singing, little Avi used to take off his little cap and bow. Thank you, he would say, for attending a performance at the Karmelicka Open Air Concert Hall. Be careful going home. This always drew a laugh.

One day, he and his mother were no longer there. They had disappeared without a trace. They and everyone else, said Jascha. What else was new? Never mind. Let me tell you a joke.

He lit two cigarettes. Cheer up, my sweetheart. Did I tell you the one about Moishe's wife? A hundred times, she replied. Oh darling, he said mournfully.

Jascha was full of jokes that he told again and again in bed and out. Soon she had heard them all a hundred times. Have you, he would say, heard the one about the Jew on the train. If she said no, he told it with great relish. Yes, she would say if she was in a certain mood, a hundred times. All right then, he would say, let's hear it. A Jew got on a train . . . she would begin. What? Not—A Jew got on a train . . . You don't know how to tell a joke. And he would tell her how the joke should begin. Carry on, he would say.

The Jew was hungry, she said. What?? He would shake his head sadly. She has no idea how to tell a joke. All right, she would say, throwing up her hands: you tell it. And happily he would begin.

Did you hear the one about the Jew crossing the border? Did you hear the one about the Jew on the train? In his jokes Jews were always crossing the border or taking a train. Their lives seemed to consist of this. Don't Jews ever do anything else? she asked him. Ho ho, many things, he replied. But not all of them are funny.

If we don't go out now, said Lilka, it will be dark. And we won't see what has become of Warsaw. Good, he said. So much the better.

———

Already the light was seeping out of the day. Snow fell from a pale sky. They huddled together for a moment beneath the hotel canopy, swathed in dark coats and fur hats. Lilka studied a map, tracing streets with a gloved finger, peering closely at the names. I don't know what's going on, she said. Have you ever heard of Solidarności Avenue or Jana Pawła II Avenue? And look at this, they've named a street after Anielewicz. That used to be Gęsia Street. And they've moved Leszno. I used to know this city inside and out. We'll be lucky if we find our way.

They stepped out into the afternoon. She squinted at the falling snow. I want to go to Marszałkowska Street. To see our apartment from before the war. Once upon a time, she told him, we had eight rooms, a conservatory, a piano. And a little bird in a cage. We had Limoges china and Oriental carpets. And a chandelier from Bohemia. The wind blew suddenly, disturbing the snow piled at the corners and crevices of the buildings, and they were covered in a shower of soft flakes. One day it was gone.

He clapped his hands together against the cold. His breath rose up in steam. You're going to be disappointed, darling. I want to go, she said. How stubborn she is, he remarked. Do you expect that Marysia will be there to greet you? That your parakeet will tweet? That the sun will shine on Warsaw? You want to ruin it for me, she said. No, my sweetheart, he replied. I want to protect you. He pulled up the collar of his coat. I'm freezing, he said. And now I have to go on this ill-fated tour. Well, come on, let's not wait until all of Warsaw freezes over.

The morning after a snowfall, said Lilka, Marysia, in slippers and a thin blouse, carrying a tub of warm water and rags, would go out on the balcony to wash the doors. The snow had climbed up the glass. Inside we were in a kind of igloo where you could barely see out. She scrubbed the glass until the outside world became visible—the cornices of the building across the way, the trees, the morning light. Why doesn't she put on a coat? said my mother. When Marysia came back in, her slippers wet, her thin pale hair clipped to her head, my mother scolded her. I'm used to it, said Marysia. We used to walk barefoot in the snow on the way to market. You're no longer in your village, said my mother. This is Warsaw.

They crossed the square. In the center was a small fountain held aloft by three stone fish, their gaping mouths filled with snow. It's just up here, said Lilka. She took his arm and pulled him forward. Jascha, she urged. We're almost there. My darling, he said, you mustn't be in such a hurry to be unhappy. The snow clung to their boots as they walked. New snow was piling up on old. A fierce wind came up and they bent forward against the force of it. Their eyes watered and their cheeks froze. The snow in Warsaw is endless, said Jascha. He pulled his scarf over his mouth as they struggled forward.

It was the Jews who had to shovel the snow, he said. Sometimes They dragged them out without coat or shoes or gloves and gave them a primitive shovel. Never mind all that, she said. Dig, Jews, They said. Dig yourselves out of the hole you're in. They were bored and They were cold. Who told them they would have to supervise Jews shoveling snow? And so even those Jews who had coats and gloves and boots were told to give them up. They were told to run with their shovels. They were told to dance with their shovels . . . We turn left here, said Lilka. She went ahead of him. Just up here, she cried.

She stood in front of her old address, staring at a square modern apartment building that had once been white. From the bare functional windows hung cheap white net curtains. It's gone, she said. Of course it's gone, replied Jascha. Everything is gone, she said. Yes, he said wearily. That's what happened. Can we go now? Wait, she said. No, I won't, he replied. It has vanished. Every sound, every face, every brick, every doorway. Staring at it won't make it come back.

My father used to take me sledding in the Krasiński Gardens . . . she began. Yes, darling, he said. Now let's go. People hurried past them silently, swathed in dark coats and heavy boots, hunched against the snow and the cold. No one looked at them. You see, he said, we're invisible. Well that makes a change. You remember how they used to study your face, your eyes, your nose, the way you walked. You can tell, they said, by the expression in their eyes. Why must the Jews always look so unhappy?

Shall we go to Krakowskie Przedmieście? The Royal
Route? she asked. And see the stage set that royal
Warsaw has become? he wanted to know. Lilka took
a small mirror out of her purse. She struggled to hold
it in front of her face and as the glass steamed up, she
applied her red lipstick. Just like your mother, he said.
Always applying her red lipstick at the most inopptune moments.

They set off down the wide Royal Route. In the open
vista that stretched out before them, pale imperial
buildings rose out of the snow on either side of the
street. The gold domes and crosses of the churches
thrust into the white sky. How beautiful, murmured
Lilka. She turned to him happily. It's just like before
the war. No, darling, said Jascha, it's not.

Look, she said, there is the Royal Palace. But why is
it so red? It wasn't like that before. It was bombed,
said Jascha. They've rebuilt it. Or tried to anyway.
The whole place looks unreal. He pulled out a white
linen handkerchief and blew his nose. I'm freezing, he

said. Let's go inside. But I want to see Nowy Świat, said Lilka. What a beautiful street it was. With elegant shops and cafes. Rebuilt, said Jascha briefly. Like a stage set, a Potemkin village. It's no longer Warsaw. This is some other confection. He pointed ahead. There's a cafe. Let's go in. I'm stiff as a corpse. But we've barely seen anything, she protested. I've seen more than enough, he informed her.

No Jews came to this part of town, he said. Verboten. Well here we are, he said. Now we can enter without risking our lives.

In the wood paneled cafe Lilka unwrapped her scarf. She shrugged out of her coat and let it fall over the back of the chair. The place was packed. People pressed up against the walls and each other. She took up the menu. Look Jascha, they have pancakes. I want one with sour cherries and whipped cream. And a hot chocolate. Also with whipped cream. Just like a courtesan, he said. That's the kind of thing they order. How would you know? she asked. I'm having a pancake with chicken and mushrooms and cream sauce, he said. Not some feminine cream puff of an order. Lilka removed her hat and pulled off her leather gloves. What a madman, she said, shaking out her thin bangle bracelets. Masculine and feminine orders.

Around them sat people swathed in layers of clothing. What do they think about, the Poles of today? she wondered. What everyone thinks about, he replied. Whether they can afford a new refrigerator. Whether the kid is doing her homework. Whether the mother-in-law is monopolizing the hot water. Jascha looked around, the place was dense with cigarette smoke. They are sitting here as though nothing ever happened. Most of them were born after the war, she replied. Look at the *babushka* in the corner, he said, and that man with the pale blue eyes and pitted face. Were they born after the war?

Jascha drank his hot chocolate and then asked for vodka. The waiter brought a bottle and two shot glasses. Jascha began to drink. How clever we were, he said.

We thought of everything. We had a thousand ways of smuggling in anything and everything. We brought in contraband through the Wall and under the Wall and over the Wall. His eyes grew bright. We filled the hearses returning from the cemetery with black-market food.

Beneath a thin layer of garbage we filled the garbage wagons with the goods. They were too fastidious to start rooting around in garbage.

He poured out another shot and drank it back. They wouldn't touch the hearses we stuffed with contraband —they were terrified of typhus. *Fleckfieber!* we would cry. We sent emaciated young children of six and seven to squeeze through the drains beneath the Wall. Sometimes they brought back too much from The Other Side. And they couldn't wiggle back in. Then we had a problem. Lilka grew pale. Shhh, she said, you're talking too loudly. People around them turned to look. Let them look, he said. What's it to me? He poured out more vodka.

Large consignments of goods were stockpiled near the Wall on The Other Side. When night fell they were thrown over into the ghetto. I had Stasik on The Other Side. He could throw over 100 sacks in less than a quarter of an hour—one every nine seconds. He smiled. We had to keep him well fed. You need a lot of strength for that. Jascha, said Lilka quietly, stop. People are staring. He poured out more vodka. Let them, he said and thrust out his chin. Do you think I care? They should all be shot, he murmured.

At the table next to them sat a woman, her pale blonde hair pulled back from her face. She stared, fascinated, at Jascha. When he looked at her, she lowered her eyes flirtatiously. She touched her mouth with her cold fingers. I'm trying to figure out where you're from, she said. Jascha looked at her out of dark heavy lidded eyes. You first, he told her. The woman shivered. Are you Polish? she asked. What do you think? Take a good look. She flushed. I don't know, she whispered. I'm from right here, said Jascha. The remarkable city of Warsaw. I got my dark eyes from my mother, a Russian princess. But I'm Polish all the same.

This is my sister, he said indicating Lilka. The woman
shook her head and forced a laugh. I don't think that's
the truth. She's very light and you're dark. She looks
Polish and you . . . Ask her, said Jascha. The woman
turned to Lilka questioningly. That's my naughty older
brother, said Lilka. I go with him to cafes so he won't
pick up too many women. The woman nodded ner-
vously. I think I will go home with this woman, said
Jascha softly. Go ahead, said Lilka.

He watched Lilka closely. She ate her pancake with
delicate bites. When she was finished, she laid down
her knife and fork and got up. I'm leaving now, she
said, and put on her coat and hat. You do what you like,
he replied and lit a cigarette.

She walked half a block before he caught up with her.
He grabbed her arm. Why do you do this? he cried. She
pulled his hand off. Did you think I would just sit there
while you seduced that Polish girl? Can't I have any fun?
he asked peevishly. Please, she replied, be my guest. He
took her arm and she shook it off. If I'm not there when

you get back, she said, I'll see you another time. Where are you going? he asked and gripped her arm. You better go back, she suggested. How long will she wait for you? You didn't wait for me at all, he said. Jascha, she said, don't start that. I didn't know. I thought you were dead. Everyone else was.

You're ruining it for me, he said. What a child, she replied. I don't want to talk to you. He walked beside her and gripped her arm tightly. Do you know what Graham Greene said about love? He called it The Ministry of Fear. As soon as you love, you fear. You have something to lose. After the war, what more was there to lose? You don't know how free that makes you. Everything has already been taken away. He held her tightly, his dark eyes on her. But you won't leave me, he said. I won't let you.

Why do you torture me? he asked. What are you talking about? she asked. You make me love you. Oh Jascha, what nonsense. She walked rapidly. And I don't want to, he said. She stopped and looked at him. He took her chin between his gloved hands. You are closer to me than my own skin, he said. She watched him. The snow fell on them.

I remember, she said at last, that Edward had an appointment with a Polish novelist by the name of J. Kroll. By then I was living with Edward in London. And working for him reading Polish novels and doing translations. I had never heard of the Polish novelist J. Kroll. Edward asked me to read the manuscript of his novel *The Way Down*. The whole thing had been handwritten in Polish on butcher's paper. Edward was intrigued. What can this be? he asked.

I turned over those waxy sheets covered in tiny handwriting, one by one. I read it without stopping. Edward asked me what I thought. Brilliant, I told him. Surreal. And black as night. A masterpiece. Make an appointment for him to come in, he said to me. I want to meet this man.

It was a Thursday afternoon in the month of June 1949, she said, blinking at the snow that fell on her lashes.

The buzzer rang and I went out to answer the door. There you stood with your dark curls and dark eyes, back from the dead. You were as thin as during the war. I felt faint. I hadn't seen you in seven years. I could barely stand. Who is J. Kroll? I asked you. What happened to Jascha Krasniewski? You smiled and shrugged. A new invention, you said. On either side of the walk the pale pink and yellow flowers stretched their slender necks toward the warmth of the sun. The birds chattered, the bees hummed in the softness of the summer afternoon. I have never, she said, neither before or since, known such happiness. He stared at her. You wicked witch, he said, you want to break my heart.

The next day, all those years ago, she had gone to his tiny London flat. I remember your flaxen hair and your blue eyes, he had said, your round arms and beautiful hands. I'm falling into a honeypot. Easy to fall into, difficult to climb out of. Through the open window the sunlight fell on her arms and her hair. She played with the thin bangles around her wrist. She saw the sunlight on his chest and watched his square fingers as they knocked a hard-boiled egg on the table and peeled off the white shell. Say my name, he said. I want to hear you say my name. I can't. Not yet. I don't know where I am, she said softly. No, he agreed. I thought I would never see you again, she had told him. Not me, he said. I knew I wasn't yet done with you, my sweetheart.

You got up from your seat and I watched you come toward me, said Lilka now. You pulled me to my feet and took me in your arms. Your skin was warm and smelled of tobacco. How strong you were. I had drunk too much and could barely stand up. Why did you give me so much, I murmured. Only a peasant drinks like that. I reached out a finger to touch your dark curls. I don't know where I am, I told you. You put your arm around my waist and led me down the hall to the bed-room. Then you carried me over the threshold. I'm going to undress you in Polish, you said, and make love to you in Polish. We'll go back to Warsaw together, my Polish sweetheart, Warsaw before the war. I was only a child, I told you. Never mind, you said. You're not anymore.

Several stars appeared in the darkening sky. The skyline grew fainter and the contours of the new Warsaw blurred. Your book came out, said Lilka, and created a sensation. You became famous overnight. Who was this handsome dark-haired refugee who had survived all this? Had these things really happened? Black as pitch, they said. Language and images so unrelenting you have to blink—or turn away. Translated into eighteen languages. Reviewed everywhere. And wherever I went there was *The Way Down* in the window of every bookshop. We had moved in together, but I barely saw you anymore.

And then you went to Frankfurt. I'm going to the Frankfurt Book Fair with Edward, he had told her, as they sat having breakfast one morning in London. It's the first Frankfurt Book Fair since the war. What better, says Edward, than to present a Jew who speaks to us from out of the ruins. Jascha bit into a poppy-seed roll. Edward says I'm going to make his name. My book, he proclaimed, will light up the night sky.

I'm going to be a famous author. He didn't tell me you
were going to Frankfurt, said Lilka. Does he tell you
everything? Jascha wanted to know. No, she answered,
of course not. And certainly not in this case because he
knows what you will say. And what is that? You'll say:
I want to go too. Well I do. But you can't, darling. It
makes no sense. And you'll distract me. I have a job to
do there. Jascha, she had said, everything will change.
Yes, he agreed. It will. Don't be sad, darling, he had
said. Nothing lasts forever.

I should be there too, Lilka had said. Aren't I the translator? They'll want to ask me about that, she went on.
No, darling, he replied, they won't. They want to meet
the author himself, not the translator. Well I could go
unofficially. He shook his head. Not this time my angel.
This is my moment. When I lay on my back on a hillside in Poland, with the cows chewing peacefully all
around me, I dreamed of the moment when my words
would fly up like a flock of birds and everyone would
know my name. Although of course it's not really my
name.

The streetlights came on and flakes drifted down over the smudged yellow globes of light. You went off to the Frankfurt Book Fair, she said to him now, and left me behind. How angry I was with you. I went to the office but I couldn't work. I could only think of the two of you at the Fair and me stuck at home. You didn't call. Edward didn't call. I sat at my desk, looking out at the bare trees, and remembered when you came the first time. Day after day I waited for news, waited for you to come back. And at last one morning Edward came. But you weren't with him.

Edward came into the office animated as I had rarely seen him. It was a triumph, he said. Even better than I imagined. They were comparing him to Kafka and Gogol. Brilliant, original, terrifying, black as night. He laughed happily. They're saying *The Way Down* might be the greatest wartime novel of them all. They couldn't praise it enough. He took out that black leather pocket notepad of his and began to read. Eighteen countries, he said. I've sold it in eighteen countries. He smiled. Not bad is it? I'm quite proud of myself.

Kroll was perfect, he said. The women fell in love with him—they all wanted to go to bed with him. And the men wanted to listen to his stories all night. He was funny and charming and just strange enough to excite them. What a character. Larger than life. He was interviewed by magazines, newspapers, even television. The man can talk. What a storyteller.

He emerged from the rubble of Warsaw, they wrote, armed only with a manuscript written on butcher's paper. It couldn't have been better. Edward's eyes shone. This is going to be Gloucester Press's biggest triumph. There's lots to do, he said. I'll want you coming in more often for the next few weeks. She had sat motionless, twisting a paperclip. Edward, she said at last, when is he coming back?

I was very angry with you, she said to him now. You didn't come home for ten days. I was out of my mind. And you slept with so many women when you were there. They saw, said Jascha, that not only did I have dark curls, but I could write. And last but not least, I had survived the war. The women thought of that boy on his own among the murderers. And immediately their breasts started dripping milk.

Did I tell you about my friend who survived Auschwitz? he had asked her. His teeth were rotten from his years in the camp, and he was as pale as though he were still stuffed into a wooden bunk there. But women loved him. They couldn't wait to go to bed with him. Jascha my friend, he told me with a wink, women love nothing more than a Polish Jew who has survived the war. When all those women with their plump thighs and eager faces offered themselves to me, how could I say no?

I don't want to hear about it, she cried. They expect it, darling, he told her. I couldn't disappoint them. No? she asked. Why not? You could have been a success without sleeping with all those women. I was intoxicated, he replied. How well would you have resisted?

In Paradise, he said to her, with the snake, as always. I thought you would be happy for me, he said. Happy that I was a sensation, that they loved my book, that Edward had sold the rights in eighteen countries. I thought you would be proud that they called me the new Kafka. But instead I find all you're thinking about is that I had a few flirtations. It's part of the game, darling. Don't you know that? I wanted you to be a success, she had said quietly. I'm very happy for you. But why did you have to betray me over and over again? It meant nothing, he protested. Call it public relations. Ach, she said to him, stop it. All those years ago he had stood up and held out his arms to her. Don't leave me darling, he said. What will I do without you? You should have thought of that at Frankfurt, she had said.

The Way Down came out in November. The reviews were ecstatic. She began to see photos of him all over the press, his dark eyes looking out slyly at the reader. He was invited everywhere. He went to parties, he spoke, he gave book signings, he was interviewed on television. He was animated by excitement all the time. Sometimes she watched him on television, in his black shirt and corduroy suit, his thick dark hair brushed back, his eyes aglow. She studied his face and his hands and looked at his eyes. He was far away. You should be happy, he told her. Your lover is a famous writer. Now he was never at home. A famous author has responsibilities, he told her.

He would disappear for days on book tours, and she didn't know when he would be back. One night she saw him on a TV talk show. She watched him, his energy too much for the small director's chair he sat in. She willed him to look at her but of course he couldn't. So Mr. Kroll, said the host, what was it like during the war? Jascha was smoking and she saw the familiar stream of smoke rising up. A picnic, a funfair, he replied. The most fun I ever had. Come come, Mr. Kroll, the host reproved him. Let's be serious. Could I be more serious? asked Jascha.

In the office Edward had said to her, if you're not happy with Kroll you can always come back to me.

Standing on Krakowskie Przedmieście, Jascha said:
And you, what did you do in the end? You slept with
that dreadful Rumanian writer. Only to pay you back,
she said. My adventures didn't mean anything, he said.
Neither did mine, she replied. Except that I found out
it went on for another six months, said Jascha. What's
good for the gander, she said, is good for the goose.
Not at all, he cried. It's not the same. You're out of the
Middle Ages, she said, if not earlier. You're out of your
mind, he said. He reached out for her. Don't touch me,
she said. He laughed. Come here, he ordered her. I'm
going to take you to bed and spank you. I'm too old for
that, she told him. Ho ho, not at all. He grabbed her.
Come here, he said, and stop all this. What a crazy
woman. It's all nearly forty years ago.

Now in the falling snow, he took her in his arms. And
God caused a deep sleep to fall upon Adam, said Jascha, and He took one of his ribs. And with the rib that
God had taken from the man, He plaited the hair of the
woman and brought her unto the man. This one at last,
bone of my bones, and flesh of my flesh, this one shall
be called woman for from man was this one taken. You

see that, said Jascha, stroking her cold face, you cannot leave me. You are part of me. Lilka looked up at him in surprise, her cheeks red with cold. Why would I leave you? she asked him. Where would I go? You are my only home. And she pressed her cold lips against his.

I'm going to write a book about you, he said. Where will you begin? she asked. I'll begin at the beginning, he replied. Once upon a time . . . she said. Not once upon a time, he replied. That's not the way to begin a story. It makes no sense. Where will you start then? she asked him. I'll start like this, he said. In the beginning Adam and Eve lived in the Garden of Eden . . . You're crazy, she cried. You can't start all the way back there. But that's where it all began, my sweetheart. The first betrayal, the first exile, the beginning of old age, the end of eternal life. Everything. I'll start there, my angel. Where you forced me to eat the forbidden fruit. Where you robbed me of eternal life. That's where our story begins. In the Garden of Eden. Must you go all the way back there? she asked. He nodded. I'm afraid so. Why are we standing out in this cold? he asked. In a moment They will order us to shovel snow.

The streetlamps came on. I cannot go to this reading, he said. She took his arm. You must, she said. That's what we came for. It was you who talked me into this madness, he said. Why did I listen to you?

———

They arrived back at the hotel frozen to the bone. Get the vodka, he told her. Vodka was invented for frigid Polish nights. Only that can warm us up. She handed him the vodka and drew a chair up to the radiator. I remember when I translated the diary of the Kaminer girl, she said. She too had been in the ghetto. But she was younger than I. And as you know, she did not survive. They found her account buried in a tin can. The writing was so tiny it had to be transcribed with a magnifying glass. You wouldn't read it, said Lilka. But there was a paragraph where she described coming up the steps on the high wooden bridge over Chłodna.

It was always packed tight with hundreds of Jews crossing from the Little to the Big Ghetto. I too had climbed those steps. I would stop at the top of that rickety bridge and gaze out at The Other Side. How beautiful it looked.

They had parks and gardens, and shops full of food. And what did we have, locked up in this filthy deadly asylum like criminals?

How I longed to be a bird and fly over there. No guards, no armbands. Just endless skies. Get a move on, they shouted. Jews, I said, let us breathe in this view of freedom for a moment. Someone kicked me from behind. Stop this sentimental nonsense, they said, we have work to do. And they shoved me forward. They were right of course. What would it get us to gaze at that most beautiful and unattainable world? It was wartime everywhere, but Over There looked like a paradise.

From our apartment we could see over to the Other Side. At least in the beginning until they boarded up the windows. I used to watch them walking down the street on The Other Side. It was another world. As

far away as the moon. One day I saw a mother and a
father with their little girl. She wore a red coat and ate
a sweet roll, scattering crumbs as she walked. Once I
had been like that little girl. Now I no longer had the
right to walk on the street. I no longer had the right
to live.

Lilka held out her glass. I told Edward I wouldn't trans-
late any more of those. They called her the Polish Anne
Frank. Irena Kaminer. And they gave me a prize for the
translation. You were in a bad mood the whole evening,
said Lilka. Yes, because I found the handwringing and
mawkishness of the proceedings absolutely disgusting, replied Jascha. I invited you to Venice on my prize
money, she said. You didn't mind that. We got lost in
the fog. Do you remember? We were wandering around
for hours. We're going to end up back in the ghetto,
you said. Only we're a few centuries too late for this
one. Not like ours. Let's have another drink, she suggested. To give you strength for the reading. I'm not
going, he said, and he lay down on the bed and piled
the pillows up beneath his head. Why should I? Make
merry with the Poles? What for?

The whole ghetto was a gauntlet, said Lilka. Squeezing through the narrow streets, people were beaten by Them on all sides. You were lucky to get through with your eyes and arms and head intact. On the days when the German we called "Frankenstein" was on duty, the number of people brought to the hospital was five or six times higher. How tireless he was, beating and shooting and whipping. If only we had had a gun.

She held out her glass. How exhausted I feel. Come to bed, he said. We'll forget the reading and everything else. We'll order up dinner and have it in bed. How about it, darling? Four courses and a dessert. But the reading, she said. Why else did we come?

He leaned over and filled their glasses. It was July 1942. *Es wird schon was kommen,* said Horowitz the Gestapo informer. Something is going to happen. You can say that again. Something was certainly going to happen. Only we didn't yet know what. And then the posters began to appear all over the ghetto. All Jews to be resettled in the East . . .

The heat was suffocating. The *Grosse Aktion* had begun. German, Polish, Jewish policemen smashed open doors and kicked the Jews out into the street. They needed 10,000 Jews a day driven to the *Umschlagplatz* for the trip to Treblinka. Guarded on every side, they pressed through the streets, carrying their bundles and suitcases, pillowcases swollen with their few remaining possessions. When the Jews had passed by, the streets were filled with pieces of broken furniture, cupboards, tables, chairs, abandoned pots and pans, discarded clothes. And everywhere the feathers that had escaped from pillows and eiderdowns. The ghetto was like a ghost town. Half the apartments deserted, their doors gaping open. A terrible heat hung over the ghetto. They were hosing down the cobblestones.

That summer, said Jascha, the city of Warsaw was not so big and it was getting smaller and smaller. The ghetto boundaries were shrinking, the apartments were emptying out. As soon as the Jews left with their bedding, in moved the Poles with new bedding. One morning a woman could no longer bear the tiny hole in which she was lodged. She climbed out on the roof with her pillow, lying flat so she couldn't be seen.

But somehow she fell asleep and began to roll. A shot rang out. The feathers of her pillow flew up into the air in a flurry of white feathers, a temporary snowfall above the city of Warsaw. And the woman rolled off the roof and fell in a tangle of limbs on the street. Who paid any attention? Another corpse? Was that anything new? The streets were full of them. We didn't see them anymore. No one even bothered to cover them with newspaper anymore. Cover me, said Jascha. I feel cold.

Why do you talk about this? asked Lilka and she pulled the eiderdown over him. Why indeed? he replied. Give me a cigarette. He left the cigarette in his mouth and inhaled. Jascha, she cried, you're holding it right next to the eiderdown. You're going to set the place on fire.

By midsummer of '42, he said, the deportations were at their height. The panic was indescribable. The Jews were trying everything imaginable to avoid the trains. The Accountant had people coming at all hours, desperate to escape, or buy their way out. Anyone not working in a German shop was to be deported. Anyone found hiding was killed on the spot. The ghetto was in chaos. Stores shut down, bakeries stopped functioning, and for the first time, smuggling stopped abruptly. Food was unattainable. The Accountant no longer slept. Get some rest, I told him. Do you think you can save every Jew in the ghetto?

Have you forgotten I was there? asked Lilka. As thousands of Jews were pressed into the walled square, we threw down white hospital gowns from the windows of the hospital that overlooked the *Umschlagplatz*. They rained down like parachutes, floating and twisting on the way. If you grabbed one and disguised yourself as a medical worker, you had a chance to get out. Nurses were running down to try to get out a parent, a brother, an aunt, a school friend. Later even a white uniform couldn't save you. Everyone was to be deported.

It was at that time, said Jascha, that a terrible error occurred. He pressed at the pillows behind his head. The Accountant kept on his payroll a hospital worker who stood at the entrance to the *Umschlagplatz*. It was his job to help out if the Accountant wanted someone pulled out at the last moment. And to report on any friends of the Accountant's who were seen coming through.

But this particular afternoon the man was called away on a medical errand. During the fifteen minutes he was away, the Accountant's wife and twin daughters passed through the gates to the *Umschlagplatz*. They had been caught up in one of the afternoon roundups. But they were not seen. And the Accountant was not informed. The man who knew every movement in the ghetto and then, at the moment when his family is taken away to die, his impeccable system of information fails. Who can understand?

People often sat there for days without food or drink, waiting to be shoved on the trains. But this time as luck would have it, it was late in the afternoon. Once the train was loaded, it left. The Accountant was informed at last and he, who never left his underground lair except to go home to his wife and daughters, ran to the *Umschlagplatz*. He had the cash. A fabulous sum. 300,000 zlotys—100,000 zlotys each, the price of buying a Jew out of the *Umschlagplatz* in the summer of 1942. But he was just too late. The train had already picked up speed. He was out of his head; he was raving. He was ready to get on a train himself. But we got him away.

For four days and nights the Accountant lay on a cot without eating or drinking. No one had ever seen him in such a state. And then, when he was left alone for a moment, he swallowed a cyanide capsule. The same capsules he sold at such high prices to those convinced that the next world was a far better place than this one.

Jascha smoked, pressing out smoke rings. And with that, he said, my smuggling career came to an end. For weeks the Accountant had been telling me to get out. What will you do without me? I asked him. We now know, he said, if we didn't before, that there is no longer any hope. As a present he handed me expensive forged identity papers in the name of Jan Kroll. The day after he died, I came out on The Other Side. Jascha drank back another glass of vodka. I owe him everything.

While the Jews were breathing their last, I pulled off my armband and came out through a tunnel to The Other Side. I was Jan Kroll now. The Accountant's former maid Tosia was waiting for me. I wore a cap pulled down low to hide my dark curls but when she saw me, she groaned. How could I hide my eyes? She took me to a room and instructed me to spend the night there. Don't show your face, she told me. Someone will come in the morning and take you to the countryside.

And who came? A peasant with a wagon who told me to get under the load of hay. There I lay in the heat, inhaling bits of straw and God knows what. The peasant stopped along the way to get something to eat and drink. I lay there for who knows how long while he drank back his vodka and slurped back his groats. Or whatever he was eating. He certainly took his time. When at last he stood beside the wagon, he murmured: are you still breathing? *Zaledwie,* I told him. Barely.

At last the wagon started up again. After what seemed like forty days and forty nights, the creaking of the wagon stopped and he told me to get out. We were in the countryside. Around us were mown fields and green hillsides. I thought I had gone blind. As though I had passed into another world. Here was silence and green and wide open space. An old peasant woman stood there smiling at me. I felt I was dreaming. Handsome boy, she said. A little dark, but never mind. She took me inside and fed me. My husband and son are gone, she said. You'll look after the cows. And milk them in the evening. Around here, she informed me, most of them have gone to Germany to work.

To her I was Marek Landowski. I know you're not Marek Landowski, she said to me, but never mind. If you pay me, you can stay. At night I played cards with the old peasant and showed her some of my magic tricks. But one day, I felt sure, the old woman would tire of all this and turn me in. I studied her pale watery eyes and wondered how long it would take.

In the morning I would lead the cows out to pasture. There I would lie on my back all day beneath the pale blue vault of the sky. The birds were singing, the clouds floated above me. They at least were not at war. I slept, I dreamed, I composed my book. The cows listened to my words with patience and understanding. I had the feeling they liked my turn of phrase. Sometimes one of them pressed her large warm face against mine. I'm the last Jew on earth, I informed her.

Lying there in that new world of sunlight and green grass, I summoned up every word, every thought, every desire, every memory. I wanted to set down all that had happened behind those Walls. I could disappear from one moment to the next, I told myself. And

I wanted them to know I carried a universe in my head. Before they shot it off.

One day, I told myself, I will be a famous author. And I will tell them how I lay on a peaceful hillside composing my book, while the city of Warsaw was in ruins and the Jews were breathing their last. I left the Jews to die, he said. You mustn't say that, she murmured. While they were mounting the trains, packed in until they couldn't breathe, I was lying on a green hillside on my own. And as far as I could see, not one of Them to bash my head in.

I was the worst milker in the world. The old lady showed me how to do it. But I couldn't pull the way she did. And I never got the rhythm right. You'll never make a farmer, she informed me. Once, as I sat milking on a small three-legged stool, the cow stomped on my foot. As though to say can't you get it right? God forgive me, he said. I left the Jews to die.

He pressed out his cigarette. My mother, he said, spoke Polish with an accent. I tried to help her get rid of it, but she couldn't. It was too late. She had been a Jew too long. Her hair was as dark as mine. And curly like mine. Her dark eyes lay in shadow. She used to bring fresh milk home in a can. And pour it out for me into a cup. Drink, my little boy, she would say. May you grow big and strong. She would buy a chicken, twist its neck, and cook a long simmering stew with carrots and onions. And we would sit together at the wooden table bent over our bowls. Mama, I would say. I have a new magic trick to show you.

One day just before she went away, she baked a cake. She wore an old apron and her hair was dusted with flour. She brought my favorite chocolate cake warm from the oven and cut me a thick slice. But I didn't want it. I wasn't hungry. Bring me an ashtray, he told Lilka. All through the war I felt guilty about it. This was before the ghetto. Even so, it wasn't easy to find chocolate powder and sugar. She had worked hard to make that cake for me. And I had refused to eat it. Sometimes late at night, as I lay in wait for the sacks to come flying over the ghetto wall, I apologized over and over again to my mother, who went away and never came back. Why hadn't I eaten that cake when I had the chance?

How happy she would be that I became a successful writer. When I was little I told her I would be a famous magician. And sitting at the kitchen table, I showed her my magic tricks. Later I told her I would be a famous writer. Already I was composing stories about chickens and rabbits and wolves and foxes in little lined notebooks. And she would indulge me by putting her hands to her cheeks and pretending to be frightened when the fox was about to eat the hen. I have never, before or since, he said, had such a good audience for my work. Lilka stared at him. As long as I've known you, this is the first time I've ever heard you talk about your mother, she said.

My mother liked my magic tricks, he said. Like the one with the egg that I would suddenly pull out from my sleeve. But when it broke she wasn't happy. There was no money to replace it. She was as modest and shy as a schoolgirl. But she found a way to feed us. And to get the little notebooks in which I jotted down all my important boyish thoughts. They shot her in the street, he said. Long before the ghetto walls went up. At home the stew she had asked me to watch till she got back was still simmering . . .

Lilka sat down beside him and took his hand. She pulled the eiderdown over his shoulders. Do you think you can comfort me? he asked. We can none of us be comforted, she replied.

Locked up behind those Walls, he said, how I longed to go back to my side of Warsaw, back to my own house. I saw it in my dreams: the coal box, the kitchen table, my parents' beds with the carved wooden headboards, my room which looked out on the courtyard. I could have walked there in ten minutes. But I didn't dare. It had become the other side of the moon. Everything is danger, darling, the whole world is danger. Even you with your soft skin and wide smile are dangerous.

Mankind is a plague. I cannot read tonight, he said. Call and tell them we're not coming.

Jascha, she said softly, I used to wait for you so impatiently. I was always afraid you would never come. I imagined you had been shot or beaten, that I would never see you again. One night I waited for you until three in the morning. I sat by the window hour after hour watching for you. It was a moonless night. The only light came from the sentry post a block away. My mother was out for the night. The streets were deserted. I was terrified that something had happened to you. And then at last I saw you. Back from the cemetery in your greatcoat and high boots, your cap pulled down low over your face, your hand over your armband to hide the whiteness. You walked close to the buildings on the other side of the street. I ran down the stairs to let you in.

Once we were upstairs you opened your "ghetto coat" with the deep pockets sewn inside. Look, you whispered and brought out a small bottle of cheap vodka from one inner pocket. And this, you said, pulling out a loaf of bread and some butter and jam from another. After we ate and drank, you laid me down on the bed. I felt the rough material of your pants against my flesh. No one ever undressed completely. Who wanted to be dragged out naked into the street?

I'm in the Garden of Eden, you said. Here? I asked. Open your legs for me darling, you said. I want to go home. And we heard the birds singing. All the birds who had fled to The Other Side, the songbirds and the swallows and the larks. Why had we not listened to them? They had shown us which way to fly. We made love soundlessly. One day, you told me, when there is no more ghetto, I will shout the house down if I want. Jascha smiled. What a romantic schoolgirl you are, he said. Come here and let me eat you up.

The snow danced before the windows, and the radiator suddenly erupted in groans. This primitive heating, said Lilka. They haven't advanced in a century. Beneath the eiderdown, Jascha turned over to light a cigarette. My father had a weakness for beggars. In the old days

when they came to the door, he would give away our
best pot, a woolen jacket that was barely worn, a good
pair of boots. Once his older sister was there. Are you
Rothschild, she cried, to give your things away like
that? What's in your head? My father shrugged. He
asked and I gave. We were always short at the end of
the month. And more than once they came and took
away the furniture to pay off a debt.

He had come to Warsaw from Radzymin. Too religious
for me there, he would say. They pray morning noon and
night and talk of their blessed rabbi non-stop. I'd rather
be with a woman any day. But when he was ready to
marry, he went back to Radzymin for a bride. It was said
he liked wild women, but he married my sweet timid
mother. She was always slightly in awe of him. He liked
that. I should have married someone like that, said Jascha. No one like that would have had you, replied Lilka.
Ha, my darling, he said, how little you know.

My father drove a dray wagon and carted things
all around Warsaw and over the bridge into Praga.

Sometimes I went with him, sitting up next to him on the high seat. He told jokes and sang songs as he held the reins in his hand. But when 1939 rolled around, even my father got serious. He stopped. Why do I talk about this now? he asked. He smoked quietly. Why now?

They ordered him to transport Jews to the ghetto in his wagon. He did it once and that was enough. The next time he said he was sick. Does this Jew look sick to you? asked one of Them. They struck him. Another one kicked him. He doesn't look sick to me. Drive, They ordered him. But by now he could barely stand. Let's see if this makes him healthier, said one and struck my father's head with the barrel of his gun.

Carefully Jascha pressed out his cigarette in the porcelain ashtray. In the wagon the Jews watched in silence. What could they do? They had a hard time calming his horses. They reared up and overturned the wagon.

I had the story from Mandel Kohner. He saw it from a doorway across the street. At first he didn't want to tell me. I forced him to. And then I went to get the body. But it had disappeared. I couldn't find where it had gone. No one seemed to know. I searched for days. He had disappeared into thin air. Like all the other Jews. And his horses and wagon. They too were never seen again. Jascha, said Lilka, you never told me this.

He loved fun. The slightest thing distracted him. He stopped for fairs and magicians and tightrope walkers and fortune tellers and pretty women. I have his eyes. And his hands. And pretty women? asked Lilka. That too.

That night Jascha put on a pair of gray flannel pants, a blue button-down shirt, a navy blue blazer. Staring at himself in the mirror, he tied an expensive silk tie she had given him. I want them to see how a proper Jew dresses, he said. You will look better than anyone, she promised him. What are you going to read? He held out his wrist to her and she fastened the small buttons of his shirt cuff. I'm going to read from *The Way Down*. The part about the young smuggler. Which part? she asked. Not his death? His death, he said. Why should I go easy on them? Why shouldn't they suffer?

Choose another part, she suggested. He was only six. And the way he dies is terrible. Let them hear it, he said. Were they blameless? Ach Lilka, don't be such a mimosa. Brush your hair, she told him. It's standing up on end.

She pulled on a red wool dress and turned for him to zip it up. She bent down to the mirror and carefully applied her red lipstick. Jascha, she said. Maybe you should read something else. What are you afraid of? he wanted to know. I'm not afraid, she replied. But why should you provoke them? Just what the Jews always said, Jascha told her. Don't provoke them, don't attract attention. She stood before him and put her hand on his arm. You know I'm not like that, she said. But what purpose does it serve now? They should know what happened, he replied.

He stared at her. Look at you, he said. You look just like a Pole. What else am I? she wanted to know. Do you think all Jews have dark curls? No, my darling, he replied. Only me. Or at least I once did. She reached up and straightened his tie. All right, he said, that's enough. Now let us go to this absurd evening in which the last Jew is asked to plead his case.

The Writers' House was packed. How strange, she murmured. Look at all these people. Do they all know of you? Of course not, he replied. They want to see what a real live Jew looks like. They haven't seen one in so many years. A small man with thinning gray hair and a nervous smile came up and greeted them, bowing. Maziewski, he introduced himself. Honored guests, he said, we are proud to welcome you. Jascha glanced at Lilka. How kind of you to invite us, said Lilka. We too are honored. He smiled and kissed her hand. What a beautiful lady, he said. You look Polish. And speak such good Polish too, he added. I am Polish, she replied. Of course, of course, he said hastily. Come with me. We will have something to drink. And then we will go into the next room for the reading.

They stood in a small reception room where plates of
hors d'oeuvres had been laid on a table covered with
a white cloth. Maziewski poured out three glasses of
vodka. Pan Kroll, he began, we are happy to welcome
back such a distinguished writer. I myself am very
much looking forward to this reading. Thank you, Pan
Maziewski, said Lilka. How kind. The three of them
raised their shot glasses. *Prosit,* they said and drank it
back. Silence fell.

Well, said Mr. Maziewski, perhaps we should go in.
Your audience is waiting, he said with a smile. Come
with me, he said. There is a seat in the front row for
Pani Kroll. And I shall lead Pan Kroll up to the stage
where I shall give a very brief introduction. Following
behind, Jascha muttered: don't be so ingratiating. I'm
just being polite, she whispered. Why? he asked. Do
they deserve it?

The elegant high-ceilinged room had cream colored
walls embossed with musical instruments of gilt. Gilt
ribbons wove their way around the violins and the

lutes. An enormous chandelier laced with gleaming rows of crystals hung from the ceiling. At the windows hung red velvet drapes. A room out of other times. Ladies and gentlemen, said Mr. Maziewski, I am proud to present to you tonight Pan Jascha Kroll, our own countryman, who has been living abroad for many years. He has had great success with his novels in Europe and America, and we are happy to welcome him back to his native land after all these years. Let us give him a round of applause.

Jascha stood before them, his chest pressed out. His white wavy hair stood up from his forehead, his dark eyes surveyed the room. They waited. But he had not finished looking. I am back in Poland, he began, after forty years. The audience began to clap. Why are you clapping? he asked coldly, and they stopped abruptly. The last time I was here, he said, I had some difficulties. They were silent. But, he went on, all this is over. Is it not? There was no response. As you know, a part of the population was shut up behind walls. They were growing increasingly uncomfortable. Several people coughed. And

when the walls came down, almost no one was left.
A man got up noisily. I won't listen to this, he said.
You can leave, said Jascha, but that doesn't change
what happened here.

I am going to read from *The Way Down,* he said. It is
the story of a young smuggler behind the Wall and
what becomes of him. He opened the book and read.
How after many adventures, the boy, as thin as a dan-
delion weed, tries to crawl through the hole beneath
the Wall to return to the ghetto with his loot. How
he becomes stuck in the middle and can neither
advance nor retreat. How a fight between those who
are starving breaks out over his contraband. How
he is beaten on both sides of the Wall until he lies
motionless . . . Why must we listen to this? cried out
a man with white hair. Wasn't it the Germans who
were responsible? It's been more than forty years,
said a woman in the front row. Most of us were not
born. A man shouted angrily—did we not suffer too?
Were we too not hungry? Did the Jews not bring it
upon themselves? suggested a woman in a tight wool
suit. People began to leave. Jascha read on. When he

had finished, five people remained. He looked up and smiled at them. Well well, he said, the small band of survivors. And he closed his book.

I had not realized, said Mr. Maziewski, that it would be so harsh. I confess I had not read your books. But your name is known in Warsaw and I thought it would be interesting to have you read to us. Our former countryman who had been away for a long time. You might have things to tell us. I did not know, he repeated, it would be quite so . . . he hesitated. We too suffered, he whispered.

I regret, he said sorrowfully, that many people left. That was not polite. Thank you for coming. Thank you, Pan Kroll. Thank you Pani Kroll. Please enjoy your stay in Warsaw. I was only a small child, he said softly. I had nothing to do with it. Jascha stared at him. No of course not, he said at last. No one had anything to do with it. Mr. Maziewski bowed his head. I wish you the best of luck, he said.

He took a handkerchief from his pocket and wiped his forehead. My wife is waiting at home, he said. She was not well enough to come. But she will want to know what happened. He put out his hand and Jascha shook it. Never mind, Pan Maziewski, he said. Go in good health. I have ordered a car for you, said Maziewski. Come with me. He motioned for them to follow him. Good night, Pan Kroll, he said. Enjoy the rest of your stay. Good night, dear lady, he said to Lilka. He smiled sheepishly. I will not tell my wife about your beauty.

They got into the taxi. Wasn't that a bit harsh? asked Lilka. Not harsh enough, he replied. Before the door was closed, the taxi began to move. The smell of alcohol hung in the interior. The driver drove quickly and the old taxi skidded in the snowy street. Hey, said Jascha, slow down. The man took a hand off the wheel and raised his palm. Not to worry, not to worry, he said and sped up. Jascha, she whispered. Stop the car, said Jascha, we're getting out here. *Nie nie,* shouted the driver loudly. I can't leave you here. How will you get back to your hotel? Look at the snow. We'll get back, replied Jascha. Let us out. The car began to swerve.

They were thrown against the seat in front. Hey, cried
Jascha. At that moment there was the sound of metal
crunching as the taxi hit another car.

The driver began to swear. Why do you distract me
while I'm driving? he cried. Now look what's happened. The driver of the other car appeared at the
window, banging with a large gloved fist, shouting for
him to open up. Now the police will be coming, said
the driver in despair. Roll down the window, cried
the man outside, and he banged again and again in a
fury.

Jascha turned to Lilka. We're getting out, he said.
I'm not waiting for the police. But Jascha, she protested. We're in the middle of nowhere. And it's
dark. He opened his door. Quick, he said, we're
getting out. Where are you going? called the driver
angrily. You have to stay. This has nothing to do
with us, replied Jascha. He and Lilka came out into
the night.

The snow was falling heavily and the air was frigid. Dear God, Jascha, she said. We don't even know where we are. Never mind, he said, I'm not getting mixed up with the police. Did you learn nothing during the war? Jascha, she said, I'm so angry with you. He took her arm. It's better this way, he said. The streetlamps were few and far between, their light dimmed by the snow. She stumbled. An icy wind stung her face. She pulled her scarf over her mouth and nose. Where are we? she asked. As they turned the corner she looked up at the street sign, half obscured by snow. Dear God in Heaven, she said. This is Grzybowska Street. We're back in the ghetto.

He stood motionless, his face alert. Well then, I know exactly where we are. The Żelazna Gate is up ahead. We continue on Grzybowska. Past Zielna and your beloved Marszałkowska. Onto Królewska. You mustn't worry. We'll soon be out. But when they came to the next crossing, he turned around in confusion. What's happened? he asked in surprise. They've changed the streets. Maybe you've forgotten, she said. Ho ho, he replied. I have forgotten nothing at all. I know every street in the ghetto. Follow me. But they had come to a dead end. The wind whipped up the snow and blew it into their faces. They bowed their heads. I don't understand, said Jascha, peering up. All right, he said after a moment, if we can't go left here, we'll take the next left. But there was no left there either.

We're lost, said Lilka. We can't get out. Lilka, he cautioned her. If I don't know every street in the ghetto, what do I know? I can't go on, said Lilka, and she pressed her face into her scarf. I'm frozen. Of course you can go on, he said. This is not the worst that ever happened to us. Yes, but now . . . Come come, he said, what has happened to my brave girl? You wouldn't have behaved like this Back There. Back There I had no choice, she said. And now? he asked.

In a moment, he stopped again. What is this street? he asked. This wasn't here before. Never mind, he said. We'll go through and see where we end up. She held tightly to his arm. The darkened streets were empty and silent. Look how deserted it is, he said. They're all gone.

At last they came out onto Bankowy Square. Ahead of them they saw the shadowy silhouettes of trees, their black branches twisted against the sky. The Saxony Gardens! said Lilka. Please, Jascha. I want to see them again. Get a postcard instead, he suggested. It's my last chance, she said. It's dark, it's bitterly cold, it's snowing, it's nighttime, said Jascha. Is this the right moment to visit a park? Come in with me, she pleaded. Just for a moment. Ach Lilka. You're driving me insane.

They entered the park. Let's sit down on a bench for a moment, she said. Like in the old days. Have you taken leave of your senses? he wanted to know. You can't sit down, you crazy woman. In this cold? You'll sit down and you won't get up. You'll freeze to death. What's the matter with you? They walked together down the allée white with snow. Jascha, she said happily, it hasn't changed. The allée was lined with classical statues that stood on tall stone plinths. Here was Summer with a basket of fruits, and Spring with garlands of flowers. Snow lay on the stone baskets and garlands of the mythical women, and collected in their stone tresses. Above them the stars lay dimmed in the night sky. Look, said Lilka, the pond is frozen solid and the swans are gone.

The Saxony Gardens, she said and her face softened. We lived nearby. I walked here with my parents every Sunday morning. Dressed in a little blue coat with velvet collar and buttons, and a little fur hat. With my mother holding one hand and my father the other, we would walk down to the lake. There we would toss pieces of stale bread to the swans who sailed down the lake two by two, their black eyes dark as night, their long bills resting on their white feathered chests. My father would say: don't let them fool you. They look so peaceful gliding along with their clean white feathers. But they are as bad tempered as camels. Even worse. And he would pinch my cheek. Even so, he would add, we will still feed them.

Lilka brushed the snow off a bench. Sit, she said. Just for a moment. I did not think I would ever again sit in these gardens. You're crazy, he said. We'll freeze. But at last he sat down beside her. There's the little gazebo, she said, pointing. Do you remember?

The snow fell from a dark sky. The white flakes settled on their hats and the shoulders of their coats as they sat staring into the park.

I came out not far from here, said Lilka. On a summer day in July of '42. How hot it was. The heat of the pavement came through your shoes. My mother had gone out the day before. She had bribed the policemen at the Grzybowska Gate. And paid a fortune for our false papers. We were Ewa and Lena Majorska. Mother and daughter. We were to meet on The Other Side at four in the afternoon. If I wasn't at Grzybowska Square, she would come back at five. The same the next day. She brushed at the snow beside her.

When I came out on the Aryan side, I could not believe my eyes. Where was I? Instead of the never ending clamor of the ghetto, the dense and desperate crowds, the filth and the misery, the trash, the endless beggars, the emaciated and dying, what did I see? Clean streets, nearly empty of people. Over here it was summer. The trees were in bloom. There were flowers. Well-dressed men and women walked in the streets, children were playing. How quiet it was. There were carriages. In the window of a store, jewelry was displayed.

I was struck dumb. My head ached; I felt completely disoriented. As though I had come to a strange and unknown place. Nothing was familiar. For a moment I was blinded. I stood as though in a dream. But passersby were stopping and staring, and I saw I would have to move quickly. There were *szmalcownicy* everywhere, blackmailers who, for a few coins, turned in Jews who had escaped the ghetto.

They surrounded me. But I wore a cross around my neck and my hair was blonder than theirs. I spoke to them in perfect Polish. What were you doing in there? they demanded to know. I showed them my small parcel wrapped in brown paper.

The Jews sewed me a dress, I said. You're a Jew, they said. How dare you, I cried. I'm going to report you. They hesitated for a moment, and then they spotted a sure thing. A woman with dark curls and a haunted expression had appeared beneath the Wall. They abandoned me and ran toward her. What did I do? I did nothing. I felt only a staggering relief that I had escaped. In those days, she said, it seemed as though you only benefited at the expense of another. You lived that they might die. You escaped that they might be caught.

And was your mother there waiting for you when you came out? asked Jascha. No, of course not. How did you know? asked Lilka. At Grzybowska Square where I had planned to meet my mother, there was Marysia.

There she stood in her cotton housedress, her wisps of pale hair pulled back with clear plastic combs. How happy I was to see her. Now, I felt sure, everything would be all right. She had brought a sweet roll for me in her basket, and I took it and ate greedily, the crumbs dropping from my mouth. Marysia, I said, and putting my arms around her small shrunken figure, I pressed my cheek against hers and my eyes filled with tears. She stroked my hair. My little one, she said. Look how thin you are.

I stared at the trees heavy with bright green leaves, shiny with sunlight. Is Mama all right? I asked. Marysia nodded. You'll see her tomorrow. Well well, said Jascha, a mother cannot come to welcome her daughter back to the land of the living. Instead she makes a date with her German friend. Far more important. You don't know that, said Lilka. He shook his head. Is this a Jewish mother?

One day in the ghetto, said Jascha, the Accountant said to me: you were seen at Cafe Hirschfeld last night. With the girl. I don't want you taking her there. Don't worry, I told him, she doesn't want to go back. She went to school with Dora Goldschmidt. Now she sees her at Cafe Hirschfeld with a red shiny mouth sitting half-naked on Kazik the smuggler's lap. She says she'll never go back. Good, said the Accountant. I don't want her there. I like her. She's a nice girl. You mean that's worse than what she sees on the streets? I asked him. That I can't do anything about, the Accountant replied. That's not under my control.

Lilka stared at him. You never told me that. Jascha shrugged. We've only been together forty years, he said. I haven't yet had time to tell you everything. He blew his nose. But I will, darling. I will.

But there's another reason I didn't take you back to Cafe Hirschfeld, he said. The tip of his cigarette glowed in the darkness. And that was because your mother went there sometimes with Keppler. Jascha, said Lilka, what are you saying? Once in a while he came into the ghetto at night, said Jascha. Some of Them did. They liked to go slumming at Cafe Hirschfeld.

There was caviar and goose-liver pate at exorbitant prices right in the ghetto. There were singers, musicians, a floor show. Anka Blum with her dark hair and red lips used to sing ballads from before the war.

German as well as Polish. The applause was thunder-
ous. The champagne flowed. It was almost real life. All
the smugglers hated your mother, he informed her.

There was a lot of scum there. But she was sleeping with
the enemy. That went beyond what they could tolerate.
But what could they do? She had high-level protection.

Jascha, said Lilka, why are you telling me this? Are you
angry at the Poles tonight? Why do you take it out on
me? Why do you torture me? He shrugged. I wanted
you to know. She turned away from him on the cold
stone bench. What a terrible man. I don't want to talk
to you. Leave me, she said. I'll go back on my own.
I'm sorry, my darling, he said. I thought you should
know. Now? she asked incredulous. For what reason? I
wanted you to know, he said, that I had nothing to do
with what happened.

And now you tell me? Why did they do it? How had
she harmed anyone? she cried. She was sleeping with

one of Them, he said. And this they couldn't tolerate. This was a betrayal they couldn't accept. They would have done better to use their bullets for the Others, said Lilka. If I had known who they were, I would have killed them myself.

It happened on a Tuesday, said Lilka. On the Other Side. She had only been out for three weeks. No one dared to tell me. Later they said the Jews had arranged it. The Jews didn't target their own. Why did they make an exception for my mother? Had she tortured anyone? Shot anyone? She turned to him. You knew about it, she said. I had nothing to do with it, he said. Why would they have involved me, knowing she was the mother of my girlfriend? It was only afterward that I was told.

Up above the moon slid out from behind white clouds. She watched him. I don't think you're telling the truth, she said. You knew. You could have warned her. She would have lived. I would have had a mother. Did we come back to dredge up all our old sorrows? asked

Jascha. To poison our relationship? Why did you bring
it up? she asked. What possessed you? I don't know,
he answered. Leave me, she said. I don't want to have
anything to do with you. I swear to you, he said. I had
nothing to do with it. Did the Accountant arrange it?
she asked. Lilka, he said wearily, the Accountant was
already dead. But he had arranged it, she said. He had
only to fix the date. And when he died one of his smugglers took on the assignment. Was it Janek? Or Itzak?
Tell me, she cried. I want to know. He sighed. Lilka,
the Accountant has been dead for forty years. What
does it matter? Well, that's my answer, she said.

In the darkness she pulled off a glove and touched her
frozen cheek. My mother, she said, this woman who
you wanted dead, did you a very great favor. Ha, replied
Jascha. I doubt that. She couldn't stand me. Your smuggler, she called me. You told me so yourself. Do you
remember that day in June 1942? she asked him. Stop
it, Lilka, he warned her. Well? she asked. The trees
stirred. Her breath rose up in circles of fog. I was at
the hospital, she said. What terrible heat. We had the
windows wide open but the air lay heavy and still. The

rooms and corridors were filled with the dying. Marek
came running to tell me you had been seen with the
others being marched to the *Umschlagplatz*. Where the
trains pulled in and the Jews disappeared.

I was out of my mind. I went from window to window
looking down on the square. But I couldn't see you
anywhere. Not surprising. Thousands of people were
squeezing into the *Umschlagplatz*. I ran to the hospital
phone. But the phone was in use and though I shouted
and cried, the man refused to get off. So I raced down
the stairs. In the square, which was now packed, I saw
some of my colleagues; doctors and nurses who were
trying to bring out a few sick Jews. I asked each one
whether they had seen you. No one had. I began to run.
I ran all the way home to my mother.

She was sitting quietly in a chair by the window. I was
nearly hysterical. She turned her cool glance on me.
So emotional, she remarked. Mama, I cried, Jascha has
gone to the *Umschlagplatz*. You must get him out. She
sighed. Do you know how much it costs these days? she

inquired. The price has gone up. She fanned herself. What terrible heat, she said. Mama, I pleaded, give it to me. I will pay you back. Even if it takes my whole life. I was sobbing. Lilka, she ordered me, pull yourself together. She brought me a glass of water and spread some jam on a piece of bread. I couldn't eat.

Mama, please. I can't do it, Lilka, she said. Do you know how much 100,000 zlotys is? And we may have to survive a while longer. I fell to my knees like a Pole. Mama, I said to her, gripping her knees, I cannot live without him. He is my life. She clicked her tongue, but I saw her gaze move away. Maybe she was remembering her love for my father. Go back to the hospital, she ordered me. But Mama . . . Go, she said.

Later I learned she had called Berndt on The Other Side, and he arranged it with a phone call. He was furious with her. He told her never to ask him something like that again. Do you think, he asked her, that I am in the business of saving Jews? My mother was very angry with me. Jascha gripped her arm. It was the Accountant who got me out. Lilka shook her head. In the end, I suppose Berndt saved Jews after all, she remarked. One Jew, said Jascha. Yes, she replied. But it was you.

For a long time they sat silently side by side on the snow covered bench. The frigid wind blew the snow against their faces. Why did you never tell me? he asked at last. Go, she said to him. I don't want you here. Lilka, he said, we have to go back. It's colder than the devil. Soon we'll be frozen. You can go, she said. I'm staying here. He turned to her in the darkness. Shall we die in Poland after all? he asked her.

———

Back at the hotel, Jascha poured out vodka. Drink darling, he said to her. Lilka sat in the armchair by the window in her coat and hat. She held out her hand mechanically for the glass. I have no feelings left, she said dully. Jascha closed the curtains. Haven't we seen enough snow? he asked her. He poured himself out another glass and drank it down. Let's go to bed, he said. I've had enough of Warsaw to last me another three lifetimes.

That night in the darkness he took her in his arms. Come to me, my darling, he said. He kissed the flesh of her throat, her mouth. How I waited for you after the war. Here is the one, said Adam to Eve, whose impending arrival rang through me like a bell all night. That was me, my sweetheart. Night after night as I waited for you. He kissed the soft skin between her legs and then knelt between them. Her thighs opened, her mouth softened and she half rose to meet him. My beloved, she murmured. He entered her with the passion of a young man. Let me come home, he cried out.

That night they were as though young again. She lay on the sheets soft and open as a young girl. Again and again he rose up and entered her. And when at last they lay breathless, their legs entwined, their skin slick with moisture, Jascha turned to her and took her in his arms. The Promised Land, he said. In the moist twisted bedclothes, they closed their eyes and slept.

It was still dark when she began shaking his shoulder. Get up, she cried, tugging at him. He awoke in terror. What is it? What is it? What's going on? he asked, his eyes wide with panic. Jascha, we have to get out! What's the matter with you? he asked, his face creased with sleep. She struggled out of bed, throwing aside the tangled sheets, and reached in the near darkness for their battered leather suitcase. I have to get out, she repeated. Otherwise it will be too late. He turned to look at her. For God's sake, Lilka, what's come over you? My heart is beating, she said. I can't catch my breath. Calm down, he said, and come back to bed.

She began pulling their clothes off the hangers and throwing them into the suitcase. Will I need this? she asked, holding up a woolen jacket. How many kilos are we allowed to take with us? Lilka, stop all this, he protested sleepily, there's plenty of time. It's still night. It's not, she said, it's six in the morning. He reached out to pull the quilt over himself. Our train is at five this

afternoon, he said. We can wait till then. Calm down.
And let me go back to sleep. He turned over.

I dreamed I was on the *Umschlagplatz,* she said, caught
up in the crowd pressing toward the train. It was a
terrible mistake. I didn't belong there. Behind me hundreds of people shoving and screaming. What a terrible
din. They were pushing me forward toward the open
car. I turned around to run and the crowd parted to let
me through. But I was paralyzed and couldn't move. I
no longer remembered how to run. The crowd looked
at me pityingly, they shook their heads. And then as
though regretfully, the crowd closed around me and
pushed me up into the train.

Not me, I cried, I'm not going. I'm still young. There
was an old man in a black coat. Grandfather, I pleaded,
I'm still young. But it was not my grandfather. He had
been shot on his way to the bookseller of Nalewki
Street. The old Jew looked at me with hooded eyes
and he shrugged. *Alles rein,* he said. Everything inside.
I was already inside. I was suffocating. And then they

slid closed the heavy wooden door and shut out the sky. And there was darkness. Grandfather, I cried.

Jascha sighed. It was a dream, he said. That's all. Now calm down. It was long ago and it's over now. He watched her throwing their clothes into the suitcase, crumpled and unfolded. He reached out a hand. Come and sit down, he said softly. She shook her head. I can't. Lilka, be reasonable. Jascha, please, she implored him. He watched her face. All right, he said at last. But we can at least have breakfast. Hurriedly she began to put on her clothes. No. We can't. There's no time. You have to get dressed. And go down and check out. We've got to be on the first train out of here. She put on her boots. There'll be a terrible crowd at the station. We want to be sure to get on. *Boże Mój,* he murmured. My God. He struggled to the bathroom, turned on the tap in the sink and washed his face with cold water.

They set off in the freezing half darkness. Warsaw lay quiet in the early morning frost. She sat stiffly against the frayed fabric of the taxi seat. Jascha sat beside her smoking, his eyes red rimmed, his chin rough with stubble. There had been no time to shave. They sat silently, watching the city roll past.

The taxi pulled up in front of the station. The driver got out and pulled their bag from the trunk. He took the money and wished them a good journey. Well well, said Lilka. At least he didn't ask us where we were from. He didn't have to ask, said Jascha. He knew.

Dawn was coming up over Warsaw. The city lay soft and silent beneath the snow. The gilded baroque domes of the churches began to glow beneath the lightening sky. What a beautiful city it was, said Lilka as they stood on the pavement. Before the war. Say goodbye to Warsaw, she said. We won't be back. I said goodbye to Warsaw forty years ago, he replied. I thought . . . she began. I know what you thought, he replied. The strangest thing, she told him, is that I have forgotten London. Forgotten our life there. Forgotten all those years. As if they never happened. It will come back to you, he told her. She bound up her hair in a knot and pulled on her fur hat. It's as though I never left Warsaw. Why, she asked him, did we have to?

They stood together on the platform. In the early light of dawn, a group of three workmen stood at the end of the platform, their toolboxes beside them. They wore rough padded jackets and pants and mangy *chapkas* on their heads; their cigarettes hung from their cold lips so they could keep their hands in their pockets.

Lilka pulled back her sleeve and looked at her watch. How brave they were, she said softly, those Jews who fought against all odds in April 1943. The women too. Even They were surprised at the courage of the Jewish women. During the eight weeks of the Ghetto Uprising, I had an irresistible longing to go back to the ghetto. I wanted to be with the Jews who were fighting Them with antiquated guns and homemade Molotov cocktails as the ghetto burned and the buildings collapsed.

The Jews had built a whole system of underground bunkers. As the ghetto burned it was nearly impossible to breathe in the underground bunkers, and those who could came out into the light of day. They fought in the sewers, in the basements, in the attics. But They were armed with incendiary bombs and tanks and flamethrowers and all manner of sophisticated weapons. And we had nothing. The Jews wanted to die fighting. How did we know They would set the whole ghetto on fire?

She tugged her scarf up around her mouth and chin. Just before Easter, I walked to the ghetto Wall. What a beautiful spring day. The sun shone, it was warm, and everywhere the trees had pressed out pale young leaves. As I came closer, I saw that beside the ghetto Wall, a funfair was in progress. There were rides, a carousel; women in thin dresses were eating doughnuts; children dressed in their Sunday best lined up for the merry-go-round. There was even a sky ride where you stepped into little cars which swung around high above the ground.

Behind the Wall, the flames leapt up into the sky. Black ash rose in the air and floated over to Our Side. As the ghetto burned, the flames rising high into the air, you could hear the screams and cries coming from the other side of the Wall. That Sunday, as the Jewish fighters burned to death in their bunkers, couples were riding high in those little cars, shrieking with laughter, riding high above the walls where they could look down and see the spectacle of the Jews dying out. I stood watching the small cars turning faster and faster. They burned the ghetto to the ground. And everyone in it. There was nothing left. Finished. Kaput. The ghetto burned for days. Even weeks later it was still smoking . . .

Ach Lilka, said Jascha. Enough.

They heard the whistle and the train, its metal sides thick with snow, came into view. He picked up their suitcase and pushed her ahead of him into the train. Go, he said to her. We don't want to be left behind.

They sat side by side in the compartment. The train lurched and began to move. When they had left the city behind, Jascha pressed back the pleated curtain and stared out the window at the endless white fields. Look, he said, a hare. He thinks he's hidden, invisible. He doesn't know I see him despite his pale camouflaged coat, despite his best efforts. And that I can flush him out at any moment. He turned to her. Have you any more of those chocolates? he asked.

We came up with all kinds of schemes to distract the German guards at the gates. Once, he said, we sent two people who could pass for workmen. They had come, we informed the Germans, to repair the policeman's booth. The door needed work. There stood our people with their wooden toolbox. They couldn't have repaired a door if their lives depended on it. We convinced the two guards that they had to go into the booth and close the door so the workmen could see how to fix it. And then, said Jascha, his cheeks shiny, while They were otherwise engaged, the driver gave the password and the wagon rolled through the gate into the ghetto. Beneath the cover lay bulging sacks of butter, oil, sugar.

He tore off the silver wrapper and pressed the chocolate into his mouth. When the #10 streetcar from The Other Side came down Zamenhofa Street, we were waiting. The driver and the conductor had been paid off. When it slowed at the turn we ran out. And pulled down linen sacks of kasha, wheat, flour, and rye that had been loaded on The Other Side. Right away we threw on sacks of bread, of knitted goods, of hand-stitched leather goods. Do you know how quick we had to be? It was a matter of seconds before the streetcar sped up again. That was in the early days, when the streetcar from The Other Side still went through the ghetto.

I was the quickest of them all, he said. And when the work was over we went to see the girls who were waiting for us. Before I met you, darling, he added. I was strong in those days. And quick. And every moment we were in danger. Women were mad for me. Were they? she asked. Sometimes I brought them something we had smuggled in. A pot of jam, a hair ribbon, a few cigarettes. What a hero I was. I still had dark curls. And I could run like the wind. He smiled. What adventures we had. He smoked and flicked the ashes onto the floor. In those days, in the ghetto, long long ago, he said, I was young.

The endless fields lay white and otherworldly in the pale winter light. Lilka took off her fur hat and laid it beside her. Before the war, she said, we had a bird. A blue and yellow parakeet in a cage. This bird was constantly cleaning itself. I used to open the door and let it out when my parents weren't home. It would fly around the room aimlessly chattering and cheeping in a high-pitched tone. Marysia would come running in and try to catch it in her dish towel. I would laugh and clap my hands as she ran in circles with the cloth and the parakeet flapped its little feathers.

She looked at him. I'll never come back, she said. No, darling, he replied, aren't you glad? It's over, she said.

Yes, my sweetheart, he said, it is. I want to go home, she said. I thought Warsaw was your home, he replied. Isn't that what you kept telling me? I have no home, she said. She stared out the window at the dark pines sagging beneath the snow. I did once but that's long ago.

I'm homeless, she said. You and all the other Polish Jews, he replied. Well never mind, he said. We'll have to do without. How can you be like that? she said. How? he asked. I've learned. London is not my home, she said. It means nothing to me. And Warsaw? he asked.

He took out a small bottle of vodka. Well well, she said in surprise, where did you get that? Drink, my angel, he said. Forget about all this. Do you remember all the tricks we used during the war to make ourselves forget? Even for a moment? He opened the bottle and handed it to her. Don't be sad, darling. All good things come to an end. She took a drink and handed the bottle back to him. He put back his head and drank. Come and sit on my lap, my sweetheart, he said, wiping his mouth. Shall I try to comfort you?

There were SS everywhere checking papers, she said. And taking away anyone who looked Jewish. They weren't very good at knowing who was a Jew and who wasn't—if they didn't have sad dark eyes and dark curls, They couldn't spot them. But the Poles knew better and could always be counted on to help. They could identify the slightest gesture, expression, way of pronouncing a word. And again and again they pointed us out, informed on us, and collected their cash.

Do you remember, she said, how our fellow Poles waited right outside the Walls, the *szmalcownicy*, ready to blackmail anyone escaping from the ghetto? How they dug up paving stones from the street beside the Wall and hurled them over to Our Side, hoping to strike a Jew? How they robbed us blind? Stripped us naked? Betrayed us to the Germans? Our own Poles. Lilka, he said, stop it. Not everyone.

Lilka pulled at the fingers of her gloves. Why did they not help us? she asked. What had we done to them? A spark from Jascha's cigarette fell on his scarf. He examined the scorched wool and scratched at it with his fingernail. They had lived with us and gone to school with us our whole lives, she said. Instead it was as though they had never known us.

Warsaw was the most beautiful city. Do you remember? Jascha smoked quietly, pressing out smoke rings in the airless compartment. Lilka, for God's sake, he said. He reached out his hand to her. Come and sit beside me, darling. Warsaw, she said, her cheeks flushed, were we not loyal to you? Did we not love you more than any other city? Our beloved Warsaw. What had we done to deserve this? Out the window the snow covered fields stretched toward an endless white horizon. A hare leapt through the snow. Warsaw, answer me.